ALISTAIR MACLEOD was born in North Battleford, Saskatchewan, in 1936. He lived on the Prairies until the age of ten when his parents moved back to the family farm on Cape Breton.

After obtaining his Teacher's Certificate from the Nova Scotia Teachers College, MacLeod took his B.A. and B.Ed. (1960) from St. Francis Xavier University, his M.A. (1961) from the University of New Brunswick, and his Ph.D. (1968) from the University of Notre Dame. He taught at Indiana University from 1966 until 1969, then moved to the University of Windsor, where he was Professor of English and Creative Writing.

MacLeod's fiction roots itself in carefully delineated and haunting settings, only to transcend the settings in humane explorations of the personal struggles that challenge and often defeat men and women of all time.

Alistair MacLeod resides in Windsor, Ontario.

THE NEW CANADIAN LIBRARY

General Editor: David Staines

Alistair MacLeod

AS BIRDS BRING
FORTH THE SUN
AND OTHER STORIES

With an Afterword by Jane Urquhart

The following dedication appeared in the original edition:
To the memory of my parents,
Alexander MacLeod and Christena MacLellan.
Tapadh Leat.

Copyright © 1986 by Alistair Macleod
Afterword copyright © 1992 by Jane Urquhart

First published in 1986 by McClelland and Stewart.
New Canadian Library edition 1992

Library and Archives Canada Cataloguing in Publication
Macleod, Alistair
As birds bring forth the sun and other stories

(New Canadian library)
Includes bibliographical references.

ISBN 978-0-7710-9882-6
I. Title. II. Series.
PS8575.L46A8 1992   C813'.54   C91-095245-0
PR9199.3.M33A8 1992

We acknowledge the financial support of the Government of Canada
through the Book Publishing Industry Development Program and that of
the Government of Ontario through the Ontario Media Development
Corporation's Ontario Book Initiative. We further acknowledge the
support of the Canada Council for the Arts and the Ontario Arts Council
for our publishing program.

All of the characters in this book are fictitious and any resemblance to
actual persons living or dead is purely coincidental.

Typesetting by M&S, Toronto
Printed and bound in Canada

McClelland & Stewart Ltd.
75 Sherbourne Street
Toronto, Ontario
M9A 2P9
www.mcclelland.com/NCL

4 5 6 7   14 13 12 11 10

Contents

The Closing Down of Summer

IT IS AUGUST now, towards the end, and the weather can no longer be trusted. All summer it has been very hot. So hot that the gardens have died and the hay has not grown and the surface wells have dried to dampened mud. The brooks that flow to the sea have dried to trickles and the trout that inhabit them and the inland lakes are soft and sluggish and gasping for life. Sometimes they are seen floating dead in the over-warm water, their bodies covered with fat grey parasites. They are very unlike the leaping, spirited trout of spring, battling and alive in the rushing, clear, cold water; so electrically filled with movement that it seems no parasite could ever lodge within their flesh.

The heat has been bad for fish and wells and the growth of green but for those who choose to lie on the beaches of the summer sun the weather has been ideal. This is a record year for tourists in Nova Scotia, we are constantly being told. More motorists have crossed the border at Amherst than ever before. More cars have landed at the ferry docks in Yarmouth. Motels and campsites have been filled to capacity. The highways are heavy with touring buses and camper trailers and cars with the inevitable lobster traps fastened to their roofs. Tourism is booming as never before.

Here on this beach, on Cape Breton's west coast, there are no tourists. Only ourselves. We have been here for most of the summer. Surprised at the endurance and consistency of the heat. Waiting for it to break and perhaps to change the spell. At the end of July we said to ourselves and to each other, "The August gale will come and shatter all of this." The August gale is the traditional storm that comes each August, the forerunner of the hurricanes that will sweep up from the Caribbean and beat and lash this coast in the months of autumn. The August gale with its shrieking winds and crashing muddied waves has generally signalled the unofficial end of summer and it may come in August's very early days. But this year, as yet, it has not come and there are only a few days left. Still we know that the weather cannot last much longer and in another week the tourists will be gone and the schools will reopen and the pace of life will change. We will have to gather ourselves together then in some way and make the decisions that we have been postponing in the back of our minds. We are perhaps the best crew of shaft and development miners in the world and we were due in South Africa on the seventh of July.

But as yet we have not gone and the telegrams from Renco Development in Toronto have lain unanswered and the telephone calls have been unreturned. We are waiting for the change in the weather that will make it impossible for us to lie longer on the beach and then we will walk, for the final time, the steep and winding zig-zagged trail that climbs the rocky face of Cameron's Point. When we reach the top of the cliff we will all be breathing heavily and then we will follow the little path that winds northward along the cliff's edge to the small field where our cars are parked, their hoods facing out to sea and their front tires scant feet from the cliffside's edge. The climb will take us some twenty minutes but we are all still in good shape after a summer of idleness.

The golden little beach upon which we lie curves in a crescent for approximately three-quarters of a mile and then terminates at either end in looming cliffs. The north cliff is called Cameron's Point after the family that once owned the land, but the south cliff has no name. Both cliffs protect the beach, slowing the winds from both north and south and preserving its tranquility.

At the south cliff a little brook ends its journey and plummets almost vertically some fifty feet into the sea. Sometimes after our swims or after lying too long in the sand we stand underneath its fall as we would a shower, feeling the fresh water fall upon our heads and necks and shoulders and running down our bodies' lengths to our feet which stand within the sea.

All of us have stood and turned our naked bodies unknown, unaccountable times beneath the spraying shower nozzles of the world's mining developments. Bodies that when free of mud and grime and the singed-hair smell of blasting powder are white almost to the colour of milk or ivory. Perhaps of leprosy. Too white to be quite healthy; for when we work we are often twelve hours in the shaft's bottom or in the development drifts and we do not often feel the sun. All summer we have watched our bodies change their colour and seen our hair grow bleached and ever lighter. Only the scars that all of us bear fail to respond to the healing power of the sun's heat. They seem to stand out even more vividly now, long running pink welts that course down our inner forearms or jagged saw-tooth ridges on the taut calves of our legs.

Many of us carry one shoulder permanently lower than the other where we have been hit by rockfalls or the lop of the giant clam that swings down upon us in the narrow closeness of the shaft's bottom. And we have arms that we cannot raise above our heads and touches of arthritis in our backs and in our shoulders, magnified by the water that chills and falls upon us in our work. Few of us have all our fingers and some have lost either eyes or ears from falling tools or discharged blasting caps or flying stone or splintering timbers. Yet it is damage to our feet that we fear most of all. For loss of toes or damage to the intricate bones of heel or ankle means that we cannot support our bodies for the gruelling twelve-hour stand-up shifts. And injury to one foot means that the other must bear double its weight, which it can do for only a short time before poor circulation sets in to numb the leg and make it too inoperative. All of us are big men, over six feet tall and near two hundred pounds, and our feet have at the best of times a great deal of pressure bearing down upon them.

We are always intensely aware of our bodies and the pains that course and twinge through them. Even late at night when we would sleep they jolt us unexpectedly as if from an electric current, bringing tears to our eyes and causing our fists to clench in the whiteness of knuckles and the biting of nails into palms. At such times we desperately shift our positions or numb ourselves from the tumblers of alcohol we keep close by our sides.

Lying now upon the beach we see the external scars on ourselves and on each other and are stirred to the memories of how they occurred. When we are clothed the price we pay for what we do is not so visible as it is now.

Beside us on the beach lie the white Javex containers filled with alcohol. It is the purest of moonshine made by our relatives back in the hills and is impossible to buy. It comes to us only as a gift or in exchange for long-past favours: bringing home of bodies, small loans of forgotten dollars, kindnesses to now-dead grandmothers. It is as clear as water, and a teaspoonful of it when touched by a match will burn with the low blue flame of a votive candle until it is completely consumed, leaving the teaspoon hot and totally dry. When we are finished here we will pour what remains into forty-ounce vodka bottles and take it with us on the long drive to Toronto. For when we decide to go we will be driving hard and fast and all of our cars are big: Cadillacs with banged-in fenders and Lincolns and Oldsmobiles. We are often stopped for speeding on the stretch outside Mt. Thom, or going through the Wentworth Valley, or on the narrow road to Fredericton, or on the fast straight road that leads from Rivière du Loup to Lévis, sometimes even on the 401. When we say that we must leave for Africa within hours we are seldom fined or in odd instances allowed to pay our speeding fines upon the spot. We do not wish to get into the entanglement of moonshine brought across provincial lines and the tedium that accompanies it. The fine for open commercial liquor is under fifteen dollars in most places and the transparent vodka bottles both show and keep their simple secret.

But we are not yet ready to leave and in the sun we pour the clear white fluid into styrofoam cups and drink it in long burning swallows, sometimes following such swallows with mouthfuls of Teem or Sprite or Seven-Up. No one bothers us here because we are so inaccessible. We can see any figure that would approach us from more than a mile away, silhouetted on the lonely cliff and the rocky and treacherous little footpath that is the only route to where we are. None of the RCMP who police this region are in any way local and it is unlikely that they even know this beach exists. And in the legal sense there is no public road that leads to the cliff where our cars now stand. Only vague paths and sheep trails through the burnt-out grass and around the clumps of alders and blueberry bushes and protruding stones and rotted stumps. The resilient young spruce trees scrape against the mufflers and oilpans of our cars and scratch against the doors. Hundreds of miles hence when we stop by the roadsides in Quebec and Ontario we will find small sprigs of this same spruce still wedged within the grillework of our cars or stuck beneath the headlight bulbs. We will remove them and take them with us to Africa as mementos or talismans or symbols of identity. Much as our Highland ancestors, for centuries, fashioned crude badges of heather or of whortleberries to accompany them on the battlefields of the world. Perhaps so that in the closeness of their work with death they might find nearness to their homes and an intensified realization of themselves. We are lying now in the ember of summer's heat and in the stillness of its time.

Out on the flatness of the sea we can see the fishermen going about their work. They do not make much money anymore and few of them take it seriously. They say that the grounds have been over-fished by the huge factory fleets from Russia, Spain and Portugal. And it is true that on the still warm nights we can see the lights of such floating factories shining brightly off the coast. They appear as strange, moveable, brilliant cities and when they are far out their blazing lights seem to mingle with those of the stars. The fishermen before us are older men or young boys. Grandfathers with their grandsons acting out their ancient rituals. At noon or at one or two before they start for home they will run their little boats into our quiet cove until their bows are almost touching the sand. They will toss us the gleaming blue-black mackerel and the silver herring and the brown-and-white striped cod and talk to us for a while, telling us anything that they think we should know. In return we toss them the whitened Javex bottles so that they may drink the pure clear contents. Sometimes the older men miss the toss and the white cylindrical bottles fall into the sea where they bob and toss like marker buoys or a child's duck in the bathtub until they are gaffed by someone in the boat or washed back in to shore. Later we cook the fish over small, crackling driftwood fires. This, we know too, cannot go on much longer.

In the quiet graveyards that lie inland the dead are buried. Behind the small white wooden churches and beneath the monuments of polished black granite they take their silent rest. Before we leave we will visit them to pray and take our last farewell. We will perhaps be afraid then, reading the dates of our brothers and uncles and cousins; recalling their youth and laughter and the place and manner of each death.

Death in the shafts and in the drifts is always violent and very often the body is so crushed or so blown apart that it cannot be reassembled properly for exposure in the coffin. Most of us have accompanied the grisly remains of such bodies trussed up in plastic bags on trains and planes and automobiles and delivered them up to the local undertaker. During the two or three days of the final wake and through the lonely all-night vigils kept in living rooms and old-fashioned parlours only memories and youthful photographs recall the physical reality that lies so dismembered and disturbed within each grey, sealed coffin. The most flattering photograph is placed upon the coffin's lid in an attempt to remind us of what was. I am thinking of this now, of the many youthful deaths I have been part of, and of the long homeward journeys in other seasons of other years. The digging of graves in the bitterness of February's cold, the shovelling of drifts of snow from the barren earth, and then the banging of the pick into the frozen ground, the striking of sparks from steel on stone and the scraping of shovels on earth and rock.

Some twenty years ago when first I went to the uranium shafts of Ontario's Elliot Lake and short-lived Bancroft we would have trouble getting our dead the final few miles to their high white houses. Often, in winter, we would have to use horses and sleighs to get them up the final hills, standing in chest-high snow, taking out window casings so that we might pass the coffin in and then out again for the last time. Or sometimes in the early spring we would again have to resort to horses when the leaving of the frost and the melting of the winter snow turned the brooks into red and roiling rivers and caused the dirt roads that led into the hills to become greasy and impassable. Sometimes in such seasons the underground springs beneath such roads erupt into tiny geysers, shooting their water upward and changing the roadbeds around them into quivering bogs that bury vehicles up to their hubs and axles.

And in November the rain is chill and cold at the graveside's edge. It falls upon our necks and splatters the red mud upon our gleaming shoes and on the pantlegs of our expensive suits. The bagpiper plays "Flowers of the Forest," as the violinist earlier played his haunting laments from the high choir loft. The music causes the hair to bristle on the backs of our necks and brings out the wildness of our grief and dredges the depths of our dense dark sorrow. At the graveside people sometimes shout farewells in Gaelic or throw themselves into the mud or upon the coffin as it is being lowered on its straps into the gaping earth.

Fifteen years ago when the timbers gave way in Springdale, Newfoundland, my younger brother died, crushed and broken amidst the constant tinkle of the dripping water and lying upon a bed of tumbled stone. We could not get him up from the bottom in time, as his eyes bulged from his head and the fluids of his body seeped quietly onto the glistening rock. Yet even as we tried we realized our task was hopeless and that he would not last, even on the surface. Would not last long enough for any kind of medical salvation. And even as the strength of his once-powerful grip began to loosen on my hand and his breath to rattle in his throat, we could see the earthly road that stretched before us as the witnesses and survivors of his death: the report to the local authorities, the statements to the company, to the police, to the coroner and then the difficult phone calls made on badly connected party lines or failing those the more efficient and more impersonal yellow telegrams. The darkness of the midnight phone call seems somehow to fade with the passing of time, or to change and be recreated like the ballads and folktales of the distant lonely past. Changing with each new telling as the tellers of the tales change, as they become different, older, more bitter or more serene. It is possible to hear descriptions of phone calls that you yourself have made some ten or fifteen years ago and to recognize very little about them except the undeniable kernel of truth that was at the centre of the messages they contained. But the yellow telegram is more blunt and more permanent in the starkness of its message and it is never, ever thrown away. It is kept in vases and in Bibles and in dresser drawers beneath white shirts and it is stumbled upon sometimes unexpectedly, years later, sometimes by other hands, in little sandalwood boxes containing locks of the baby's hair or tucked inside the small shoes in which he learned to walk. A simple obituary of a formal kind.

When my brother died in Springdale, Newfoundland, it was the twenty-first of October and when we brought his body home we were already deep into fall. On the high hardwood hills the mountain ash and the aspen and the scarlet maple were ablaze with colour beneath the weakened rays of the autumn sun. On alternate days the rain fell; sometimes becoming sleet or small hard hailstones. Sometimes the sun would shine in the morning, giving way to the vagaries of precipitation in the afternoon. And sometimes the cloud cover would float over the land even as the sun shone, blocking the sun out temporarily and casting shadows as if a giant bird were passing overhead. Standing beneath such a gliding cloud and feeling its occasional rain we could see the sun shining clearly at a distance of only a mile away. Seeing warmth so reachably near while feeling only the cold of the icy rain. But at the digging of his grave there was no sun at all. Only the rain falling relentlessly down upon us. It turned the crumbling clay to the slickest of mud, as slippery and glistening as that of the potter's wheel but many times more difficult to control. When we had dug some four feet down, the earthen walls began to slide and crumble and to give way around us and to fall upon our rubber boots and to press against the soaking pantlegs that clung so clammily to our blue-veined legs. The deeper we dug the more intensely the rain fell, the drops dripping from our eyebrows and from our noses and the icy trickles running down the backs of our necks and down our spines and legs and into our squishing and sucking boots. When we had almost reached the required depth one of the walls that had been continuously crumbling and falling suddenly collapsed and with a great whoosh rolled down upon us. We were digging in our traditional family plot and when the wall gave way it sent the box that contained my father's coffin rolling down upon us. He had been dead for five years then, blown apart in Kirkland Lake, and at the time of his burial his coffin had been sealed. We were wildly and irrationally frightened by the slide and braced our backs against the splintered and disintegrating box, fearful lest it should tip and fall upon us and spill and throw whatever rotting relics remained of that past portion of our lives. Of little flesh but maybe green decaying bones or strands of silver matted hair.

We had held it there, braced by our backs in the pouring rain, until timbers were brought to shore up the new grave's side and to keep the past dead resting quietly. I had been very frightened then, holding the old dead in the quaking mud so that we might make room for the new in that same narrow cell of sliding earth and cracking wood. The next day at his funeral the rain continued to fall and in the grave that received him the unsteady timbers and the ground they held so temporarily back seemed but an extension of those that had caused his life to cease.

Lying now in the precarious heat of this still and burning summer I would wish that such thoughts and scenes of death might rise like the mists from the new day's ocean and leave me dry and somehow emptied on this scorching fine-grained sand.

In Africa it will be hot too, in spite of the coming rainy season, and on the veldt the heat will shimmer and the strange, fine-limbed animals will move across it in patterns older than memory. The nomads will follow their flocks of bleating goats in their constant search for grass and moisture and the women will carry earthen jars of water on their heads or baskets of clothes to slap against the rocks where the water is found.

In my own white house my wife does her declining wash among an increasingly bewildering battery of appliances. Her kitchen and her laundry room and her entire house gleam with porcelain and enamel and an ordered cleanliness that I can no longer comprehend. Little about me or about my work is clean or orderly and I am always mildly amazed to find the earnings of the violence and dirt in which I make my living converted into such meticulous brightness. The lightness of white and yellow curtains rustling crisply in the breeze. For us, most of our working lives are spent in rough, crude bunk-houses thrown up at the shafthead's site. Our bunks are made of two-by-fours sometimes roughly hammered together by ourselves and we sleep two men to a room or sometimes four or sometimes in the development's early stages in the vast "ram pastures" of twenty or thirty or perhaps even forty men crowded together in one vast, rectangular, unpartitioned room. Such rooms are like hospital wards without the privacy of the dividing curtains and they are filled, constantly, day and night, with the sounds of men snoring and coughing or spitting into cans by their bedsides, the incoherent moans and mumbles of uneasy sleepers and the thuds of half-conscious men making groaning love to their passive pillows. In Africa we will sleep, mostly naked, under incongruous structures of mosquito netting, hearing the sometimes rain on the roofs of corrugated iron. In the near 24-hour winter darkness of the Yukon, we have slept in sleeping bags, weighted down with blankets and surrounded by various heaters, still to wake to our breath as vapour in the coldness of the flashlight's gleam.

It is difficult to explain to my wife such things and we have grown more and more apart with the passage of the years. Meeting infrequently now almost as shy strangers, communicating mostly over vast distances through ineffectual say-nothing letters or cheques that substitute money for what once was conceived as love. Sometimes the cheques do not even come from me for in the developing African nations the political situation is often uncertain and North American money is sometimes suddenly and almost whimsically "frozen" or "nationalized," making it impossible to withdraw or remove. In times and places of such uneasiness, shaft crews such as ours often receive little or no actual money, only slips of paper to show our earnings, which are deposited in the metropolitan banks of New York or Toronto or London and from which our families are issued monthly cheques.

I would regain what was once real or imagined with my wife. The long nights of passionate lovemaking that seemed so short, the creating and birth of our seven children. Yet I was never home for the birth of any of my children, only for their fathering. I was not home when two of them died so shortly after birth and I have not been home to participate or to share in many of the youthful accomplishments of the other five. I have attended few parents' nights or eighth-grade graduations or father-and-son hockey banquets, and broken tricycle wheels and dolls with crippled limbs have been mended by other hands than mine.

Now my wife seems to have gone permanently into a world of avocado appliances and household cleanliness and vicarious experiences provided by the interminable soap operas that fill her television afternoons. She has perhaps gone as deeply into that life as I have into the life of the shafts, seeming to tunnel ever downward and outward through unknown depths and distances and to become lost and separated and unavailable for communication. Yet we are not surprised or critical of each other for she too is from a mining family and grew up largely on funds sent home by an absentee father. Perhaps we are but becoming our previous generation.

And yet there are times, even now, when I can almost physically feel the summer of our marriage and of our honeymoon and of her singing the words of the current popular songs into my then-attentive ears. I had been working as part of a crew in Uranium City all winter and had been so long without proper radio reception that I knew nothing of the music of that time's hit parade. There was always a feeling of mild panic then, on hearing whole dance floors of people singing aloud songs that had come and flourished since my departure and which I had never heard. As if I had been on a journey to the land of the dead.

It would be of little use now to whisper popular lyrics into my ears for I have become partially deaf from the years of the jackleg drill's relentless pounding into walls of constant stone. I cannot hear much of what my wife and children say to me and communicate with the men about me through nods and gestures and the reading of familiar lips. Musically, most of us have long abandoned the modern hit parades and have gone, instead, back to the Gaelic songs remembered from our early youth. It is these songs that we hum now on the hotness of this beach and which we will take with us on our journey when we go.

We have perhaps gone back to the Gaelic songs because they are so constant and unchanging and speak to us as the privately familiar. As a youth and as a young man I did not even realize that I could understand or speak Gaelic and entertained a rather casual disdain for those who did. It was not until the isolation of the shafts began that it began to bubble up somehow within me, causing a feeling of unexpected surprise at finding it there at all. As if it had sunk in unconsciously through some strange osmotic process while I had been unwittingly growing up. Growing up without fully realizing the language of the conversations that swirled around me. Now in the shafts and on the beach we speak it almost constantly though it is no longer spoken in our homes. There is a "Celtic Revival" in the area now, fostered largely by government grants, and the younger children are taught individual

Gaelic words in the classrooms for a few brief periods during each month. It is a revival that is very different from our own and it seems, like so much else, to have little relevance for us and to have largely passed us by. Once, it is true, we went up to sing our Gaelic songs at the various Celtic concerts which have become so much a part of the summer culture and we were billed by the bright young schoolteachers who run such things as MacKinnon's Miners' Chorus; but that too seemed as lonely and irrelevant as it was meaningless. It was as if we were parodies of ourselves, standing in rows, wearing our miners' gear, or being asked to shave and wear suits, being plied with rum while waiting for our turn on the program, only then to mouth our songs to batteries of tape recorders and to people who did not understand them. It was as if it were everything that song should not be, contrived and artificial and non-spontaneous and lacking in communication.

I have heard and seen the Zulus dance until they shook the earth. I have seen large splendid men leap and twist and bend their bodies to the hard-baked flatness of the reddened soil. And I have followed their gestures and listened to their shouts and looked into their eyes in the hope that I might understand the meaning of their art. Hoping to find there a message that is recognizable only to primitive men. Yet, though I think I have caught glimpses of their joy, despair or disdain, it seems that in the end they must dance mainly for themselves. Their dancing speaks a language whose true meaning will elude me forever; I will never grasp the full impact of the subtleties and nuances that are spoken by the small head gesture or the flashing fleck of muscle.

I would like to understand more deeply what they have to say in the vague hope that it might be in some way akin to what is expressed in our own singing. That there might be some message that we share. But I can never enter deeply enough into their experience, can never penetrate behind the private mysteries of their eyes. Perhaps, I think sometimes, I am expecting too much. Yet on those occasions when we did sing at the concerts, I would have liked to reach beyond the tape recorders and the faces of the uninvolved to something that might prove to be more substantial and enduring. Yet in the end it seemed we too were only singing to ourselves. Singing songs in an archaic language as we too became more archaic and recognizing the nods of acknowledgement and shouted responses as coming only from our own friends and relatives. In many cases the same individuals from whom we had first learned our songs. Songs that are for the most part local and private and capable of losing almost all of their substance in translation. Yet in the introduction to the literature text that my eldest daughter brings home from university it states that "the private experience, if articulated with skill, may communicate an appeal that is universal beyond the limitations of time or landscape." I have read that over several times and thought about its meaning in relation to myself.

When I was a boy my father told me that I would never understand the nature of sex until I had participated in it in some worthwhile way, and that there was little point in trying to grasp its meaning through erotic reading or looking at graphic pictures or listening to the real or imagined experiences of older men. As if the written or the spoken word or the mildly pornographic picture were capable of reaching only a small portion of the distance it might hope to journey on the road to understanding. In the early days of such wistful and exploratory reading the sexual act seemed most frequently to be described as "like flying." A boggling comparison at the time to virginal young men who had never been airborne. In the future numbness of our flight to Africa we will find little that is sexual if it is to be like our other flights to such distant destinations.

We will not have much to say about our flight to those we leave behind and little about our destinations when we land. Sending only the almost obligatory postcards that talk about the weather continents and oceans away. Saying that "things are going as expected," "going well." Postcards that have as their most exciting feature the exotic postage stamps sought after by the younger children for games of show and tell.

I have long since abandoned any hope of describing the sexual act or having it described to me. Perhaps it is enough to know that it is not at all like flying, though I do not know what it is really like. I have never been told, nor can I, in my turn, tell. But I would like somehow to show and tell the nature of my work and perhaps some of my entombed feelings to those that I would love, if they would care to listen.

I would like to tell my wife and children something of the way my years pass by on the route to my inevitable death. I would like to explain somehow what it is like to be a gladiator who fights always the impassiveness of water as it drips on darkened stone. And what it is like to work one's life in the tightness of confined space. I would like somehow to say how I felt when I lost my father in Kirkland Lake or my younger brother in Springdale, Newfoundland. I would like to say how frightened I am sometimes of what I do. And of how I lie awake at night aware of my own decline and of the diminishing of the men around me. For all of us know we will not last much longer and that it is unlikely we will be replaced in the shaft's bottom by members of our own flesh and bone. For such replacement, like our Gaelic, seems to be of the past and now largely over.

Our sons will go to the universities to study dentistry or law and to become fatly affluent before they are thirty. Men who will stand over six feet tall and who will move their fat, pudgy fingers over the limited possibilities to be found in other people's mouths. Or men who sit behind desks shuffling papers relating to divorce or theft or assault or the taking of life. To grow prosperous from pain and sorrow and the desolation of human failure. They will be far removed from the physical life and will seek it out only through jogging or golf or games of handball with friendly colleagues. They will join expensive private clubs for the pleasures of perspiration and they will not die in falling stone or chilling water or thousands of miles from those they love. They will not die in any such manner, partially at least because we have told them not to and have encouraged them to seek out other ways of life which lead, we hope, to gentler deaths. And yet because it seems they will follow our advice instead of our lives, we will experience, in any future that is ours, only an increased sense of anguished isolation and an ironic feeling of confused bereavement. Perhaps it is always so for parents who give the young advice and find that it is followed. And who find that those who follow such advice must inevitably journey far from those who give it to distant lonely worlds which are forever unknowable to those who wait behind. Yet perhaps those who go find in the regions to which they travel but another kind of inarticulate loneliness. Perhaps the dentist feels mute anguish as he circles his chair, and the lawyer who lives in a world of words finds little relationship between professional talk and what he would hope to be true expression. Perhaps he too in his quiet heart sings something akin to Gaelic songs, sings in an old archaic language private words that reach to no one. And perhaps both lawyer and dentist journey down into an Africa as deep and dark and distant as ours. I can but vaguely imagine what I will never know.

I have always wished that my children could see me at my work. That they might journey down with me in the dripping cage to the shaft's bottom or walk the eerie tunnels of the drifts that end in walls of staring stone. And that they might see how articulate we are in the accomplishment of what we do. That they might appreciate the perfection of our drilling and the calculation of our angles and the measuring of our powder, and that they might understand that what we know through eye and ear and touch is of a finer quality than any information garnered by the most sophisticated of mining engineers with all their elaborate equipment.

I would like to show them how professional we are and how, in spite of the chill and the water and the dark and the danger, there is perhaps a certain eloquent beauty to be found in what we do. Not the beauty of stillness to be found in gleaming crystal or in the polished hardwood floors to which my wife devotes such care but rather the beauty of motion on the edge of violence, which by its very nature can never long endure. It is perhaps akin to the violent motion of the huge professional athletes on the given days or nights of their many games. Men as huge and physical as are we; polished and eloquent in the propelling of their bodies towards their desired goals and in their relationships and dependencies on one another but often numb and silent before the microphones of sedentary interviewers. Few of us get to show our children what we do on national television; we offer only the numbness and silence by itself. Unable either to show or tell.

I have always wished to be better than the merely mediocre and I have always wanted to use the power of my body in the fulfilling of such a wish. Perhaps that is why I left the university after only one year. A year which was spent mainly as an athlete and as a casual reader of English literature. I could not release myself enough physically and seemed always to be constricted and confined. In sleeping rooms that were too low, by toilet stalls that were too narrow, in lecture halls that were too hot, even by the desks in those lecture halls, which I found always so difficult to get in and out of. Confined too by bells and buzzers and curfews and deadlines, which for me had little meaning. I wanted to burst out, to use my strength in some demanding task that would allow me somehow to feel that I was breaking free. And I could not find enough release in the muddy wars on the football field or in the thudding contact of the enclosed and boarded rink. I suppose I was drawn too by the apparent glamour of the men who followed the shafts. Impressed by their returning here in summer with their fast cars and expensive clothes; also by the fact that I was from a mining family that has given itself for generations to the darkened earth.

I was aware even then of the ultimate irony of my choice. Aware of how contradictory it seemed that someone who was bothered by confinement should choose to spend his working days in the most confined of spaces. Yet the difference seems to be that when we work we are never still. Never merely entombed like the prisoner in the passive darkness of his solitary confinement. For we are always expanding the perimeters of our seeming incarceration. We are always moving downward or inward or forward or in the driving of our raises even upward. We are big men engaged in perhaps the most violent of occupations and we have chosen as our adversary walls and faces of massive stone. It is as if the stone of the spherical earth has challenged us to move its weight and find its treasure and we have accepted the challenge and responded with drill and steel and powder and strength and all our ingenuity. In the chill and damp we have given ourselves to the breaking down of walls and barriers. We have sentenced ourselves to enclosures so that we might taste the giddy joy of breaking through. Always hopeful of breaking through though we know we never will break free.

Drilling and hammering our way to the world's resources, we have left them when found and moved on. Left them for others to expand or to exploit and to make room for the often stable communities that come in our wake: the sewer lines and the fire hydrants and the neat rows of company houses; the over-organized athletic leagues and the ever-hopeful schools; the Junior Chambers of Commerce. We have moved about the world, liberating resources, largely untouched by political uncertainties and upheavals, seldom harmed by the midnight plots, the surprising coups and the fast assassinations. We were in Haiti with Duvalier in 1960 and in Chile before Allende and in the Congo before it became associated with Zaire. In Bolivia and Guatemala and in Mexico and in a Jamaica that the tourists never see. Each segment of the world aspires to the treasure, real or imagined, that lies encased in its vaults of stone, and those who would find such booty are readily admitted and handsomely paid, be they employed by dictator or budding democracy or capitalists expanding their holdings and their wealth. Renco Development on Bay Street will wait for us. They will endure our summer on the beach and our lack of response to their seemingly urgent messages. They will endure our Toronto drunkenness and pay our bail and advance us personal loans. And when we go they will pay us thousands of dollars for our work, optimistically hoping that they may make millions in their turn. They will wait for us because they know from years of many contracts that we are the best bet to deliver for them in the end.

There are two other crews in Canada as strong, perhaps even stronger than we are. They are in Rouyn-Noranda; and as our crew is known as MacKinnon, theirs are known by the names of Lafrenière and Picard. We have worked beside them at various times, competed with them and brawled with them in the hall-like beer parlours of Malarctic and Temiskaming, and occasionally we have saved one another's lives. They will not go to Africa for Renco Development because they are imprisoned in the depths of their language. And because they speak no English they will not move out of Quebec or out of northern or north-eastern Ontario. Once there was also the O'Leary crew, who were Irish Newfoundlanders. But many of them were lost in a cave-in in India, and of those who remained most have gone to work with their relatives on high-steel construction in New York. We see them sometimes, now, in the bars of Brooklyn or sometimes in the summers at the ferry terminal in North Sydney before they cross to Port-aux-Basques. Iron work, they say, also pays highly for the risk to life; and the long fall from the towering, swaying skyscrapers can occur for any man but once. It seems, for them, that they have exchanged the possibility of being fallen upon for that of falling itself. And that after years of dodging and fearing falling objects from above, they have become such potential objects themselves. Their loss diminishes us too because we know how good they were at what they did, and know too that the mangled remnants of their dead were flown from India in sealed containers to lie on such summer days as these beneath the nodding wild flowers that grow on outport graves.

I must not think too much of death and loss, I tell myself repeatedly. For if I am to survive I must be as careful and calculating with my thoughts as I am with my tools when working so far beneath the earth's surface. I must always be careful of sloppiness and self-indulgence lest they cost me dearly in the end.

Out on the ocean now it is beginning to roughen and the southwest wind is blowing the smallish waves into larger versions of themselves. They are beginning to break upon the beach with curling whitecaps at their crests and the water that they consist of seems no longer blue but rather a dull and sombre grey. There are no longer boats visible on the once-flat sea, neither near at hand nor on the horizon's distant line. The sun no longer shines with the fierceness of the earlier day and the sky has begun to cloud over. Evening is approaching. The sand is whipped by the wind and blows into our faces and stings our bodies as might a thousand pinpricks or the tiny tips of many scorching needles. We flinch and shake ourselves and reach for our protective shirts. We leave our prone positions and come restlessly to our feet, coughing and spitting and moving uneasily like nervous animals anticipating a storm. In the sand we trace erratic designs and patterns with impatient toes. We look at one another, arching our eyebrows like bushy question marks. Perhaps this is what we have been waiting for? Perhaps this is the end and the beginning?

And now I can feel the eyes of the men upon me. They are waiting for me to give interpretations of the signals, waiting for my sign. I hesitate for a moment, running my eyes along the beach, watching water touching sand. And then I nod my head. There is almost a collective sigh that is more sensed than really heard. Almost like distant wind in far-off trees. Then suddenly they begin to move. Rapidly they gather their clothes and other belongings, shaking out the sand, folding and packing. Moving swiftly and with certainty they are closing down their summer even as it is closing down on them. MacKinnon's miners are finished now and moving out. We are leaving the beach of the summer sun and perhaps some of us will not see it anymore. For some of us may not return alive from the Africa for which we leave.

We begin to walk. First along the beach towards the north cliff of Cameron's Point, and then up the steep and winding zig-zagged trail that climbs its face. When I am halfway up I stop and look back at the men strung out in single file behind me. We are mountain climbers in our way though bound together by no physical ropes of any kind. They stop and look back too; back and down to the beach we have so recently vacated. The waves are higher now and are breaking and cresting and rolling farther in. They have obliterated the outlines of our bodies in the sand and our footprints of brief moments before already have been washed away. There remains no evidence that we have ever been. It is as if we have never lain, nor ever walked nor ever thought what thoughts we had. We leave no art or mark behind. The sea has washed its sand slate clean.

And then the rain begins to fall. Not heavily but almost hesitantly. It is as if it has been hot and dry for so long that the act of raining has almost been forgotten and has now to be slowly and almost painfully relearned.

We reach the summit of the cliff and walk along the little path that leads us to our cars. The cars are dusty and their metal is still hot from the earlier sun. We lean across their hoods to lift the windshield wipers from the glass. The rubber of the wiper blades has almost melted into the windshields because of heat and long disuse, and when we lift them slender slivers of rubber remain behind. These blades will have to be replaced.

The isolated raindrops fall alike on windshield and on roof, on hood and trunk. They trace individual rivulets through the layers of grime and then trickle down to the parched and waiting earth.

And now it is two days later. The rain has continued to fall and in it we have gone about preparing and completing our rituals of farewell. We have visited the banks and checked out all the dates on our insurance policies. And we have gathered our working clothes, which when worn continents hence will make us loom even larger than we are in actual life. As if we are Greek actors or mastodons of an earlier time. Soon to be replaced or else perhaps to be extinct.

We have stood bareheaded by the graves and knelt in the mud by the black granite stones. And we have visited privately and in tiny self-conscious groups the small white churches which we may not see again. As we have become older it seems we have become strangely more religious in ways that border close on superstition. We will take with us worn family rosaries and faded charms and loop ancestral medals and crosses of delicate worn fragility around our scar-lashed necks and about the thickness of our wrists, seemingly unaware of whatever irony they might project. This too seems but a further longing for the past, far removed from the "rational" approaches to religion that we sometimes encounter in our children.

We have said farewells to our children too and to our wives and I have offered kisses and looked into their eyes and wept outwardly and inwardly for all I have not said or done and for my own clumsy failure at communication. I have not been able, as the young say, "to tell it like it is," and perhaps now I never shall.

By four o'clock we are ready to go. Our cars are gathered with their motors running and we will drive them hard and fast and be in Toronto tomorrow afternoon. We will not stop all night except for a few brief moments at the gleaming service stations and we will keep one sober and alert driver at the wheel of each of our speeding cars. Many of the rest of us will numb ourselves with moonshine for our own complex and diverse reasons: perhaps to loosen our thoughts and tongues or perhaps to deaden and hold them down; perhaps to be as the patient who takes an anaesthetic to avoid operational pain. We will hurtle in a dark night convoy across the landscapes and the borders of four waiting provinces.

As we move out, I feel myself a figure in some mediaeval ballad who has completed his formal farewells and goes now to meet his fatalistic future. I do not particularly wish to feel this way and again would shake myself free from thoughts of death and self-indulgence.

As we gather speed the land of the seacoast flashes by. I am in the front seat of the lead car, on the passenger side next to the window. In the side mirror I can see the other cars stretched out behind us. We go by the scarred and abandoned coal workings of our previous generations and drive swiftly westward into the declining day. The men in the back seat begin to pass around their moonshine and attempt to adjust their long legs within the constricted space. After a while they begin to sing in Gaelic, singing almost unconsciously the old words that are so worn and so familiar. They seem to handle them almost as they would familiar tools. I know that in the other cars they are doing the same even as I begin silently to mouth the words myself. There is no word in Gaelic for goodbye, only for farewell.

More than a quarter of a century ago in my single year at

university, I stumbled across an anonymous lyric from the fifteenth century. Last night while packing my clothes I encountered it again, this time in the literature text of my eldest daughter. The book was very different from the one that I had so casually used, as different perhaps as is my daughter from me. Yet the lyric was exactly the same. It had not changed at all. It comes to me now in this speeding car as the Gaelic choruses rise around me. I do not particularly welcome it or want it and indeed I had almost forgotten it. Yet it enters now regardless of my wants or wishes, much as one might see out of the corner of the eye an old acquaintance one has no wish to see at all. It comes again, unbidden and unexpected and imperfectly remembered. It seems borne up by the mounting, surging Gaelic voices like the flecked white foam on the surge of the towering, breaking wave. Different yet similar, and similar yet different, and in its time unable to deny:

> *I wend to death, knight stith in stour;*
> *Through fight in field I won the flower;*
> *No fights me taught the death to quell –*
> *I wend to death, sooth I you tell.*

> *I wend to death, a king iwis;*
> *What helpes honour or worlde's bliss?*
> *Death is to man the final way –*
> *I wende to be clad in clay.*

Winter Dog

I AM WRITING this in December. In the period close to Christmas, and three days after the first snowfall in this region of southwestern Ontario. The snow came quietly in the night or in the early morning. When we went to bed near midnight, there was none at all. Then early in the morning we heard the children singing Christmas songs from their rooms across the hall. It was very dark and I rolled over to check the time. It was 4:30 a.m. One of them must have awakened and looked out the window to find the snow and then eagerly awakened the others. They are half crazed by the promise of Christmas, and the discovery of the snow is an unexpected giddy surprise. There was no snow promised for this area, not even yesterday.

"What are you doing?" I call, although it is obvious.

"Singing Christmas songs," they shout back with equal obviousness, "because it snowed."

"Try to be quiet," I say, "or you'll wake the baby."

"She's already awake," they say. "She's listening to our singing. She likes it. Can we go out and make a snowman?"

I roll from my bed and go to the window. The neighbouring houses are muffled in snow and silence and there are as yet no lights in any of them. The snow has stopped falling and its whitened quietness reflects the shadows of the night.

"This snow is no good for snowmen," I say. "It is too dry."

"How can snow be dry?" asks a young voice. Then an older one says, "Well, then can we go out and make the first tracks?"

They take my silence for consent and there are great sounds of rustling and giggling as they go downstairs to touch the light switches and rummage and jostle for coats and boots.

"What on earth is happening?" asks my wife from her bed. "What are they doing?"

"They are going outside to make the first tracks in the snow," I say. "It snowed quite heavily last night."

"What time is it?"

"Shortly after 4:30."

"Oh."

We ourselves have been nervous and restless for the past weeks. We have been troubled by illness and uncertainty in those we love far away on Canada's east coast. We have already considered and rejected driving the fifteen hundred miles. Too far, too uncertain, too expensive, fickle weather, the complications of transporting Santa Claus.

Instead, we sleep uncertainly and toss in unbidden dreams. We jump when the phone rings after 10:00 p.m. and are then reassured by the distant voices.

"First of all, there is nothing wrong," they say. "Things are just the same."

Sometimes we make calls ourselves, even to the hospital in Halifax, and are surprised at the voices which answer.

"I just got here this afternoon from Newfoundland. I'm going to try to stay a week. He seems better today. He's sleeping now."

At other times we receive calls from farther west, from Edmonton and Calgary and Vancouver. People hoping to find objectivity in the most subjective of situations. Strung out in uncertainty across the time zones from British Columbia to Newfoundland.

Within our present city, people move and consider possibilities:

If he dies tonight we'll leave right away. Can you come?

We will have to drive as we'll never get air reservations at this time.

I'm not sure if my car is good enough. I'm always afraid of the mountains near Cabano.

If we were stranded in Rivière du Loup we would be worse off than being here. It would be too far for anyone to come and get us.

My car will go but I'm not so sure I can drive it all the way. My eyes are not so good anymore, especially at night in drifting snow.

Perhaps there'll be no drifting snow.

There's always drifting snow.

We'll take my car if you'll drive it. We'll have to drive straight through.

John phoned and said he'll give us his car if we want it or he'll drive – either his own car or someone else's.

He drinks too heavily, especially for long-distance driving, and at this time of year. He's been drinking ever since this news began.

He drinks because he cares. It's just the way he is.

Not everybody drinks.

Not everybody cares, and if he gives you his word, he'll never drink until he gets there. We all know that.

But so far nothing has happened. Things seem to remain the same.

Through the window and out on the white plane of the snow, the silent, laughing children now appear. They move in their muffled clothes like mummers on the whitest of stages. They dance and gesture noiselessly, flopping their arms in parodies of heavy, happy, earthbound birds. They have been warned by the eldest to be aware of the sleeping neighbours so they cavort only in pantomime, sometimes raising mittened hands to their mouths to suppress their joyous laughter. They dance and prance in the moonlight, tossing snow in one another's direction, tracing out various shapes and initials, forming lines which snake across the previously unmarked whiteness. All of it in silence, unknown and unseen and unheard to the neighbouring world. They seem unreal even to me, their father, standing at his darkened window. It is almost as if they have danced out of the world of folklore like happy elves who cavort and mimic and caper through the private hours of this whitened dark, only to vanish with the coming of the morning's light and leaving only the signs of their activities behind. I am tempted to check the recently vacated beds to confirm what perhaps I think I know.

Then out of the corner of my eye I see him. The golden collie-like dog. He appears almost as if from the wings of the stage or as a figure newly noticed in the lower corner of a winter painting. He sits quietly and watches the playful scene before him and then, as if responding to a silent invitation, bounds into its midst. The children chase him in frantic circles, falling and rolling as he doubles back and darts and dodges between their legs and through their outstretched arms. He seizes a mitt loosened from its owner's hand, and tosses it happily in the air and then snatches it back into his jaws an instant before it reaches the ground and seconds before the tumbling bodies fall on the emptiness of its expected destination. He races to the edge of the scene and lies facing them, holding the mitt tantalizingly between his paws, and then as they dash towards him, he leaps forward again, tossing and catching it before him and zig-zagging through them as the Sunday football player might return the much sought-after ball. After he has gone through and eluded them all, he looks back over his shoulder and again, like an elated athlete, tosses the mitt high in what seems like an imaginary end zone. Then he seizes it once more and lopes in a wide circle around his pursuers, eventually coming closer and closer to them until once more their stretching hands are able to actually touch his shoulders and back and haunches, although he continues always to wriggle free. He is touched but never captured, which is the nature of the game. Then he is gone. As suddenly as he came. I strain my eyes in the direction of the adjoining street, towards the house where I have often seen him, always within a yard enclosed by woven links of chain. I see the flash of his silhouette, outlined perhaps against the snow or the light cast by the street lamps or the moon. It arcs upwards and seems to hang for an instant high above the top of the fence and then it descends on the other side. He lands on his shoulder in a fluff of snow and with a half roll regains his feet and vanishes within the shadow of his owner's house.

"What are you looking at?" asks my wife.

"That golden collie-like dog from the other street was just playing with the children in the snow."

"But he's always in that fenced-in yard."

"I guess not always. He jumped the fence just now and went back in. I guess the owners and the rest of us think he's fenced in but he knows he's not. He probably comes out every night and leads an exciting life. I hope they don't see his tracks or they'll probably begin to chain him."

"What are the children doing?"

"They look tired now from chasing the dog. They'll probably soon be back in. I think I'll go downstairs and wait for them and make myself a cup of coffee."

"Okay."

I look once more towards the fenced-in yard but the dog is nowhere to be seen.

I first saw such a dog when I was twelve and he came as a pup of about two months in a crate to the railroad station which was about eight miles from where we lived. Someone must have phoned or dropped in to say: "Your dog's at the station."

He had come to Cape Breton in response to a letter and a cheque which my father had sent to Morrisburg, Ontario. We had seen the ads for "cattle collie dogs" in the *Family Herald*, which was the farm newspaper of the time, and we were in need of a good young working dog.

His crate was clean and neat and there was still a supply of dog biscuits with him and a can in the corner to hold water. The baggage handlers had looked after him well on the trip east, and he appeared in good spirits. He had a white collar and chest and four rather large white paws and a small white blaze on his forehead. The rest of him was a fluffy, golden brown, although his eyebrows and the tips of his ears as well as the end of his tail were darker, tingeing almost to black. When he grew to his full size the blackish shadings became really black, and although he had the long, heavy coat of a collie, it was in certain areas more grey than gold. He was also taller than the average collie and with a deeper chest. He seemed to be at least part German Shepherd.

It was winter when he came and we kept him in the house where he slept behind the stove in a box lined with an old coat. Our other dogs slept mostly in the stables or outside in the lees of woodpiles or under porches or curled up on the banking of the house. We seemed to care more for him because he was smaller and it was winter and he was somehow like a visitor; and also because more was expected of him and also perhaps because we had paid money for him and thought about his coming for some time – like a "planned" child. Sceptical neighbours and relatives who thought the idea of paying money for a dog was rather exotic or frivolous would ask: "Is that your Ontario dog" or "Do you think your Ontario dog will be any good?"

He turned out to be no good at all and no one knew why. Perhaps it was because of the suspected German Shepherd blood. But he could not "get the hang of it." Although we worked him and trained him as we had other dogs, he seemed always to bring panic instead of order and to make things worse instead of better. He became a "head dog," which meant that instead of working behind the cattle he lunged at their heads, impeding them from any forward motion and causing them to turn in endless, meaningless bewildered circles.

On the few occasions when he did go behind them, he was "rough," which meant that instead of being a floating, nipping, suggestive presence, he actually bit them and caused them to gallop, which was another sin. Sometimes in the summer the milk cows suffering from his misunderstood pursuit would jam pell mell into the stable, tossing their wide horns in fear, and with their great sides heaving and perspiring while down their legs and tails the wasted milk ran in rivulets mingling with the blood caused by his slashing wounds. He was, it was said, "worse than nothing."

Gradually everyone despaired, although he continued to grow grey and golden and was, as everyone agreed, a "beautiful-looking dog."

He was also tremendously strong and in the winter months I would hitch him to a sleigh which he pulled easily and willingly on almost any kind of surface. When he was harnessed I used to put a collar around his neck and attach a light line to it so that I might have some minimum control over him, but it was hardly ever needed. He would pull home the Christmas tree or the bag of flour or the deer which was shot far back in the woods; and when we visited our winter snares he would pull home the gunnysacks which contained the partridges and rabbits which we gathered. He would also pull us, especially on the flat windswept stretches of land beside the sea. There the snow was never really deep and the water that oozed from a series of fresh-water springs and ponds contributed to a glaze of ice and crisply crusted snow which the sleigh runners seemed to sing over without ever breaking through. He would begin with an easy lope and then increase his swiftness until both he and the sleigh seemed to touch the surface at only irregular intervals. He would stretch out then with his ears flattened against his head and his shoulders bunching and contracting in the rhythm of his speed. Behind him on the sleigh we would cling tenaciously to the wooden slats as the particles of ice and snow dislodged by his nails hurtled towards our faces. We would avert our heads and close our eyes and the wind stung so sharply that the difference between freezing and burning could not be known. He would do that until late in the afternoon when it was time to return home and begin our chores.

On the sunny winter Sunday that I am thinking of, I planned to visit my snares. There seemed no other children around that afternoon and the adults were expecting relatives. I harnessed the dog to the sleigh, opened the door of the house and shouted that I was going to look at my snares. We began to climb the hill behind the house on our way to the woods when we looked back and out towards the sea. The "big ice," which was what we called the major pack of drift ice, was in solidly against the shore and stretched out beyond the range of vision. It had not been "in" yesterday, although for the past weeks we had seen it moving offshore, sometimes close and sometimes distant, depending on the winds and tides. The coming of the big ice marked the official beginning of the coldest part of winter. It was mostly drift ice from the Arctic and Labrador, although some of it was fresh-water ice from the estuary of the St. Lawrence. It drifted down with the dropping temperatures, bringing its own mysterious coldness and stretching for hundreds of miles in craters and pans, sometimes in grotesque shapes and sometimes in dazzling architectural forms. It was blue and white and sometimes grey and at other times a dazzling emerald green.

The dog and I changed our direction towards the sea, to find what the ice might yield. Our land had always been beside the sea and we had always gone towards it to find newness and the extraordinary; and over the years we, as others along the coast, had found quite a lot, although never the pirate chests of gold which were supposed to abound or the reasons for the mysterious lights that our elders still spoke of and persisted in seeing. But kegs of rum had washed up, and sometimes bloated horses and various fishing paraphernalia and valuable timber and furniture from foundered ships. The door of my room was apparently the galley door from a ship called the *Judith Franklin* which was wrecked during the early winter in which my great-grandfather was building his house. My grandfather told of how they had heard the cries and seen the lights as the ship neared the rocks and of how they had run down in the dark and tossed lines to the people while tying themselves to trees on the shore. All were saved, including women clinging to small children. The next day the builders of the new house went down to the shore and salvaged what they could from the wreckage of the vanquished ship. A sort of symbolic marriage of the new and the old: doors and shelving, stairways, hatches, wooden chests and trunks and various glass figurines and lanterns which were miraculously never broken.

People came too. The dead as well as the living. Bodies of men swept overboard and reported lost at sea and the bodies of men still crouched within the shelter of their boats' broken bows. And sometimes in late winter young sealers who had quit their vessels would walk across the ice and come to our doors. They were usually very young – some still in their teens – and had signed on for jobs they could not or no longer wished to handle. They were often disoriented and did not know where they were, only that they had seen land and had decided to walk towards it. They were often frostbitten and with little money and uncertain as to how they might get to Halifax. The dog and I walked towards the ice upon the sea.

Sometimes it was hard to "get on" the ice, which meant that at the point where the pack met the shore there might be open water or irregularities caused by the indentations of the coastline or the workings of the tides and currents, but for us on that day there was no difficulty at all. We were "on" easily and effortlessly and enthused in our new adventure. For the first mile there was nothing but the vastness of the white expanse. We came to a clear stretch where the ice was as smooth and unruffled as that of an indoor arena and I knelt on the sleigh while the dog loped easily along. Gradually the ice changed to an uneven terrain of pressure ridges and hummocks, making it impossible to ride farther; and then suddenly, upon rounding a hummock, I saw the perfect seal. At first I thought it was alive, as did the dog who stopped so suddenly in his tracks that the sleigh almost collided with his legs. The hackles on the back of his neck rose and he growled in the dangerous way he was beginning to develop. But the seal was dead, yet facing us in a frozen perfection that was difficult to believe. There was a light powder of snow over its darker coat and a delicate rime of frost still formed the outline of its whiskers. Its eyes were wide open and it stared straight ahead towards the land. Even now in memory it seems more real than reality – as if it were transformed by frozen art into something more arresting than life itself. The way the sudden seal in the museum exhibit freezes your eyes with the touch of truth. Immediately I wanted to take it home.

It was frozen solidly in a base of ice so I began to look for something that might serve as a pry. I let the dog out of his harness and hung the sleigh and harness on top of the hummock to mark the place and began my search. Some distance away I found a pole about twelve feet long. It is always surprising to find such things on the ice field but they are, often amazingly, there, almost in the same way that you might find a pole floating in the summer ocean. Unpredictable but possible. I took the pole back and began my work. The dog went off on explorations of his own.

Although it was firmly frozen, the task did not seem impossible and by inserting the end of the pole under first one side and then the other and working from the front to the back, it was possible to cause a gradual loosening. I remember thinking how very warm it was because I was working hard and perspiring heavily. When the dog came back he was uneasy, and I realized it was starting to snow a bit but I was almost done. He sniffed with disinterest at the seal and began to whine a bit, which was something he did not often do. Finally, after another quarter of an hour, I was able to roll my trophy onto the sleigh and with the dog in harness we set off. We had gone perhaps two hundred yards when the seal slid free. I took the dog and the sleigh back and once again managed to roll the seal on. This time I took the line from the dog's collar and tied the seal to the sleigh, reasoning that the dog would go home anyway and there would be no need to guide him. My fingers were numb as I tried to fasten the awkward knots and the dog began to whine and rear. When I gave the command he bolted forward and I clung at the back of the sleigh to the seal. The snow was heavier now and blowing in my face but we were moving rapidly and when we came to the stretch of arena-like ice we skimmed across it almost like an iceboat, the profile of the frozen seal at the front of the sleigh like those figures at the prows of Viking ships. At the very end of the smooth stretch, we went through. From my position at the end of the sleigh I felt him drop almost before I saw him, and rolled backwards seconds before the sleigh and seal followed him into the blackness of the water. He went under once carried by his own momentum but surfaced almost immediately with his head up and his paws scrambling at the icy, jagged edge of the hole; but when the weight and momentum of the sleigh and its burden struck, he went down again, this time out of sight.

I realized we had struck a "seam" and that the stretch of smooth ice had been deceivingly and temporarily joined to the rougher ice near the shore and now was in the process of breaking away. I saw the widening line before me and jumped to the other side just as his head miraculously came up once more. I lay on my stomach and grabbed his collar in both my hands and then in a moment of panic did not know what to do. I could feel myself sliding towards him and the darkness of the water and was aware of the weight that pulled me forward and down. I was also aware of his razor-sharp claws flailing violently before my face and knew that I might lose my eyes. And I was aware that his own eyes were bulging from their sockets and that he might think I was trying to choke him and might lunge and slash my face with his teeth in desperation. I knew all of this but somehow did nothing about it; it seemed almost simpler to hang on and be drawn into the darkness of the gently slopping water, seeming to slop gently in spite of all the agitation. Then suddenly he was free, scrambling over my shoulder and dragging the sleigh behind him. The seal surfaced again, buoyed up perhaps by the physics of its frozen body or the nature of its fur. Still looking more genuine than it could have in life, its snout and head broke the open water and it seemed to look at us curiously for an instant before it vanished permanently beneath the ice. The loose and badly tied knots had apparently not held when the sleigh was in a near-vertical position and we were saved by the ineptitude of my own numbed fingers. We had been spared for a future time.

He lay gasping and choking for a moment, coughing up the icy salt water, and then almost immediately his coat began to freeze. I realized then how cold I was myself and that even in the moments I had been lying on the ice, my clothes had begun to adhere to it. My earlier heated perspiration was now a cold rime upon my body and I imagined it outlining me there, beneath my clothes, in a sketch of frosty white. I got on the sleigh once more and crouched low as he began to race towards home. His coat was freezing fast, and as he ran the individual ice-coated hairs began to clack together like rhythmical castanets attuned to the motion of his body. It was snowing quite heavily in our faces now and it seemed to be approaching dusk, although I doubted if it were so on the land which I could now no longer see. I realized all the obvious things I should have considered earlier. That if the snow was blowing in our faces, the wind was off the land, and if it was off the land, it was blowing the ice pack back out to sea. That was probably one reason why the seam had opened. And also that the ice had only been "in" one night and had not had a chance to "set." I realized other things as well. That it was the time of the late afternoon when the tide was falling. That no one knew where we were. That I had said we were going to look at snares, which was not where we had gone at all. And I remembered now that I had received no answer even to that misinformation, so perhaps I had not even been heard. And also if there was drifting snow like this on land, our tracks would by now have been obliterated.

We came to a rough section of ice: huge slabs on their sides and others piled one on top of the other as if they were in some strange form of storage. It was no longer possible to ride the sleigh but as I stood up I lifted it and hung on to it as a means of holding on to the dog. The line usually attached to his collar had sunk with the vanished seal. My knees were stiff when I stood up; and deprived of the windbreak effect which the dog had provided, I felt the snow driving full into my face, particularly my eyes. It did not merely impede my vision, the way distant snow flurries might, but actually entered my eyes, causing them to water and freeze nearly shut. I was aware of the weight of ice on my eyelashes and could see them as they gradually lowered and became heavier. I did not remember ice like this when I got on, although I did not find that terribly surprising. I pressed the soles of my numb feet firmly down upon it to try and feel if it was moving out, but it was impossible to tell because there was no fixed point of reference. Almost the sensation one gets on a conveyor belt at airports or on escalators; although you are standing still you recognize motion, but should you shut your eyes and be deprived of sight, even that recognition may become ambiguously uncertain.

The dog began to whine and to walk around me in circles, binding my legs with the traces of the harness as I continued to grasp the sleigh. Finally I decided to let him go as there seemed no way to hold him and there was nothing else to do. I unhitched the traces and doubled them up as best I could and tucked them under the backpad of his harness so they would not drag behind him and become snagged on any obstacles. I did not take off my mitts to do so as I was afraid I would not be able to get them back on. He vanished into the snow almost immediately.

The sleigh had been a gift from an uncle, so I hung on to it and carried it with both hands before me like an ineffectual shield against the wind and snow. I lowered my head as much as I could and turned it sideways so the wind would beat against my head instead of directly into my face. Sometimes I would turn and walk backwards for a few steps. Although I knew it was not the wisest thing to do, it seemed at times the only way to breathe. And then I began to feel the water sloshing about my feet.

Sometimes when the tides or currents ran heavily and the ice began to separate, the water that was beneath it would well up and wash over it almost as if it were reflooding it. Sometimes you could see the hard ice clearly beneath the water but at other times a sort of floating slush was formed mingling with snow and "slob" ice which was not yet solid. It was thick and dense and soupy and it was impossible to see what lay beneath it. Experienced men on the ice sometimes carried a slender pole so they could test the consistency of the footing which might or might not lie before them, but I was obviously not one of them, although I had a momentary twinge for the pole I had used to dislodge the seal. Still, there was nothing to do but go forward.

When I went through, the first sensation was almost of relief and relaxation for the water initially made me feel much warmer than I had been on the surface. It was the most dangerous of false sensations for I knew my clothes were becoming heavier by the second. I clung to the sleigh somewhat as a raft and lunged forward with it in a kind of up-and-down swimming motion, hoping that it might strike some sort of solidity before my arms became so weighted and sodden that I could no longer lift them. I cried out then for the first time into the driving snow.

He came almost immediately, although I could see he was afraid and the slobbing slush was up to his knees. Still, he seemed to be on some kind of solid footing for he was not swimming. I splashed towards him and when almost there, desperately threw the sleigh before me and lunged for the edge of what seemed like his footing, but it only gave way as if my hands were closing on icy insubstantial porridge. He moved forward then, although I still could not tell if what supported him would be of any use to me. Finally I grasped the breast strap of his harness. He began to back up then, and as I said, he was tremendously strong. The harness began to slide forward on his shoulders but he continued to pull as I continued to grasp and then I could feel my elbows on what seemed like solid ice and I was able to hook them on the edge and draw myself, dripping and soaking, like another seal out of the black water and onto the whiteness of the slushy ice. Almost at once my clothes began to freeze. My elbows and knees began to creak when I bent them as if I were a robot from the realm of science fiction and then I could see myself clothed in transparent ice as if I had been coated with shellac or finished with clear varnish.

As the fall into the winter sea had at first seemed ironically warm, so now my garments of ice seemed a protection against the biting wind, but I knew it was a deceptive sensation and that I did not have much time before me. The dog faced into the wind and I followed him. This time he stayed in sight, and at times even turned back to wait for me. He was cautious but certain and gradually the slush disappeared, and although we were still in water, the ice was hard and clear beneath it. The frozen heaviness of my clothes began to weigh on me and I could feel myself, ironically, perspiring within my suit of icy armour. I was very tired, which I knew was another dangerous sensation. And then I saw the land. It was very close and a sudden surprise. Almost like coming upon a stalled and unexpected automobile in a highway's winter storm. It was only yards away, and although there was no longer any ice actually touching the shore, there were several pans of it floating in the region between. The dog jumped from one to the other and I followed him, still clutching the sleigh, and missing only the last pan which floated close to the rocky shore. The water came only to my waist and I was able to touch the bottom and splash noisily on land. We had been spared again for a future time and I was never to know whether he had reached the shore himself and come back or whether he had heard my call against the wind.

We began to run towards home and the land lightened and there were touches of evening sun. The wind still blew but no snow was falling. Yet when I looked back, the ice and the ocean were invisible in the swirling squalls. It was like looking at another far and distant country on the screen of a snowy television.

I became obsessed, now that I could afford the luxury, with not being found disobedient or considered a fool. The visitors' vehicles were still in the yard so I imagined most of the family to be in the parlour or living room, and I circled the house and entered through the kitchen, taking the dog with me. I was able to get upstairs unnoticed and get my clothes changed and when I came down I mingled with everybody and tried to appear as normal as I could. My own family was caught up with the visitors and only general comments came my way. The dog, who could not change his clothes, lay under the table with his head on his paws and he was also largely unnoticed. Later as the ice melted from his coat, a puddle formed around him, which I casually mopped up. Still later someone said, "I wonder where that dog has been, his coat is soaking wet." I was never to tell anyone of the afternoon's experience or that he had saved my life.

Two winters later I was sitting at a neighbour's kitchen table when I looked out the window and saw the dog as he was shot. He had followed my father and also me and had been sitting rather regally on a little hill beside the house and I suppose had presented an ideal target. But he had moved at just the right or wrong time and instead of killing him the high-powered bullet smashed into his shoulder. He jumped into the air and turned his snapping teeth upon the wound, trying to bite the cause of the pain he could not see. And then he turned towards home, unsteady but still strong on three remaining legs. No doubt he felt, as we all do, that if he could get home he might be saved, but he did not make it, as we knew he could not, because of the amount of blood on the snow and the wavering pattern of his three-legged tracks. Yet he was, as I said, tremendously strong and he managed almost three-quarters of a mile. The house he sought must have been within his vision when he died for we could see it quite clearly when we came to his body by the roadside. His eyes were open and his tongue was clenched between his teeth and the little blood he had left dropped red and black on the winter snow. He was not to be saved for a future time anymore.

I learned later that my father had asked the neighbour to shoot him and that we had led him into a kind of ambush. Perhaps my father did so because the neighbour was younger and had a better gun or was a better shot. Perhaps because my father did not want to be involved. It was obvious he had not planned on things turning out so messy.

The dog had become increasingly powerful and protective, to the extent that people were afraid to come into the yard. And he had also bitten two of the neighbour's children and caused them to be frightened of passing our house on their journeys to and from school. And perhaps there was also the feeling in the community that he was getting more than his share of the breeding: that he travelled farther than other dogs on his nightly forays and that he fought off and injured the other smaller dogs who might compete with him for female favours. Perhaps there was fear that his dominance and undesirable characteristics did not bode well for future generations.

This has been the writing down of a memory triggered by the sight of a golden dog at play in the silent snow with my own excited children. After they came in and had their hot chocolate, the wind began to blow; and by the time I left for work, there was no evidence of their early-morning revels or any dog tracks leading to the chain-link fence. The "enclosed" dog looked impassively at me as I brushed the snow from the buried windshield. What does he know? he seemed to say.

The snow continues to drift and to persist as another uncertainty added to those we already have. Should we be forced to drive tonight, it will be a long, tough journey into the wind and the driving snow which is pounding across Ontario and Quebec and New Brunswick and against the granite coast of Nova Scotia. Should we be drawn by death, we might well meet our own. Still, it is only because I am alive that I can even consider such possibilities. Had I not been saved by the golden dog, I would not have these tight concerns or children playing in the snow or of course these memories. It is because of him that I have been able to come this far in time.

It is too bad that I could not have saved him as well and my feelings did him little good as I looked upon his bloodied body there beside the road. It was too late and out of my control and even if I had known the possibilities of the future it would not have been easy.

He was with us only for a while and brought his own changes, and yet he still persists. He persists in my memory and in my life and he persists physically as well. He is there in this winter storm. There in the golden-grey dogs with their black-tipped ears and tails, sleeping in the stables or in the lees of woodpiles or under porches or curled beside the houses which face towards the sea.

To Every Thing There Is a Season

I AM SPEAKING *here of a time when I was eleven and lived with my family on our small farm on the west coast of Cape Breton. My family had been there for a long, long time and so it seemed had I. And much of that time seems like the proverbial yesterday. Yet when I speak on this Christmas 1977, I am not sure how much I speak with the voice of that time or how much in the voice of what I have since become. And I am not sure how many liberties I may be taking with the boy I think I was. For Christmas is a time of both past and present and often the two are imperfectly blended. As we step into its nowness we often look behind.*

We have been waiting now, it seems, forever. Actually, it has been most intense since Halloween when the first snow fell upon us as we moved like muffled mummers upon darkened country roads. The large flakes were soft and new then and almost generous and the earth to which they fell was still warm and as yet unfrozen. They fell in silence into the puddles and into the sea where they disappeared at the moment of contact. They disappeared, too, upon touching the heated redness of our necks and hands or the faces of those who did not wear masks. We carried our pillowcases from house to house, knocking on doors to become silhouettes in the light thrown out from kitchens (white pillowcases held out by whitened forms). The snow fell between us and the doors and was transformed in shimmering golden beams. When we turned to leave, it fell upon our footprints and as the night wore on obliterated them and all the records of our movements. In the morning everything was soft and still and November had come upon us.

My brother Kenneth, who is two and a half, is unsure of his last Christmas. It is Halloween that looms largest in his memory as an exceptional time of being up late in magic darkness and falling snow. "Who are you going to dress up as at Christmas?" he asks. "I think I'll be a snowman." All of us laugh at that and tell him Santa Claus will find him if he is good and that he need not dress up at all. We go about our appointed tasks waiting for it to happen.

I am troubled myself about the nature of Santa Claus and I am trying to hang on to him in any way that I can. It is true that at my age I no longer *really* believe in him yet I have hoped in all his possibilities as fiercely as I can; much in the same way, I think, that the drowning man waves desperately to the lights of the passing ship on the high sea's darkness. For without him, as without the man's ship, it seems our fragile lives would be so much more desperate.

My mother has been fairly tolerant of my attempted perpetuation. Perhaps because she has encountered it before. Once I overheard her speaking about my sister Anne to one of her neighbours. "I thought Anne would *believe* forever," she said. "I practically had to tell her." I have somehow always wished I had not heard her say that as I seek sanctuary and reinforcement even in an ignorance I know I dare not trust.

Kenneth, however, believes with an unadulterated fervour, and so do Bruce and Barry who are six-year-old twins. Beyond me there is Anne who is thirteen and Mary who is fifteen, both of whom seem to be leaving childhood at an alarming rate. My mother has told us that she was already married when she was seventeen, which is only two years older than Mary is now. That too seems strange to contemplate and perhaps childhood is shorter for some than it is for others. I think of this sometimes in the evenings when we have finished our chores and the supper dishes have been cleared away and we are supposed to be doing our homework. I glance sideways at my mother, who is always knitting or mending, and at my father, who mostly sits by the stove coughing quietly with his handkerchief at his mouth. He has "not been well" for over two years and has difficulty breathing whenever he moves at more than the slowest pace. He is most sympathetic of all concerning my extended hopes and says we should hang on to the good things in our lives as long as we are able. As I look at him out of the corner of my eye, it does not seem that he has many of them left. He is old, we think, at forty-two.

Yet Christmas, in spite of all the doubts of our different ages, is a fine and splendid time, and now as we pass the midpoint of December our expectations are heightened by the increasing coldness that has settled down upon us. The ocean is flat and calm and along the coast, in the scooped-out coves, has turned to an icy slush. The brook that flows past our house is almost totally frozen and there is only a small channel of rushing water that flows openly at its very centre. When we let the cattle out to drink, we chop holes with the axe at the brook's edge so that they can drink without venturing onto the ice.

The sheep move in and out of their lean-to shelter restlessly stamping their feet or huddling together in tightly packed groups. A conspiracy of wool against the cold. The hens perch high on their roosts with their feathers fluffed out about them, hardly feeling it worthwhile to descend to the floor for their few scant kernels of grain. The pig, who has little time before his butchering, squeals his displeasure to the cold and with his snout tosses his wooden trough high in the icy air. The splendid young horse paws the planking of his stall and gnaws the wooden cribwork of his manger.

We have put a protective barricade of spruce boughs about

our kitchen door and banked our house with additional boughs and billows of eel grass. Still, the pail of water we leave standing in the porch is solid in the morning and has to be broken with the hammer. The clothes my mother hangs on the line are frozen almost instantly and sway and creak from their suspending clothespins like sections of dismantled robots: the stiff-legged rasping trousers and the shirts and sweaters with unyielding arms outstretched. In the morning we race from our frigid upstairs bedrooms to finish dressing around the kitchen stove.

We would extend our coldness half a continent away to the Great Lakes of Ontario so that it might hasten the Christmas coming of my oldest brother, Neil. He is nineteen and employed on the "lake boats," the long flat carriers of grain and iron ore whose season ends any day after December 10, depending on the ice conditions. We wish it to be cold, cold on the Great Lakes of Ontario, so that he may come home to us as soon as possible. Already his cartons have arrived. They come from different places: Cobourg, Toronto, St. Catharines, Welland, Windsor, Sarnia, Sault Ste. Marie. Places that we, with the exception of my father, have never been. We locate them excitedly on the map, tracing their outlines with eager fingers. The cartons bear the lettering of Canada Steamship Lines, and are bound with rope knotted intricately in the fashion of sailors. My mother says they contain his "clothes" and we are not allowed to open them.

For us it is impossible to know the time or manner of his coming. If the lakes freeze early, he may come by train because it is cheaper. If the lakes stay open until December 20, he will have to fly because his time will be more precious than his money. He will hitchhike the last sixty or hundred miles from either station or airport. On our part, we can do nothing but listen with straining ears to radio reports of distant ice formations. His coming seems to depend on so many factors which are out there far beyond us and over which we lack control.

The days go by in fevered slowness until finally on the morning of December 23 the strange car rolls into our yard. My mother touches her hand to her lips and whispers "Thank God." My father gets up unsteadily from his chair to look through the window. Their longed-for son and our golden older brother is here at last. He is here with his reddish hair and beard and we can hear his hearty laugh. He will be happy and strong and confident for us all.

There are three other young men with him who look much the same as he. They too are from the boats and are trying to get home to Newfoundland. They must still drive a hundred miles to reach the ferry at North Sydney. The car seems very old. They purchased it in Thorold for two hundred dollars because they were too late to make any reservations, and they have driven steadily since they began. In northern New Brunswick their windshield wipers failed but instead of stopping they tied lengths of cord to the wipers' arms and passed them through the front window vents. Since that time, in whatever precipitation, one of them has pulled the cords back and forth to make the wipers function. This information falls tiredly but excitedly from their lips and we greedily gather it in. My father pours them drinks of rum and my mother takes out her mincemeat and the fruitcakes she has been carefully hoarding. We lean on the furniture or look from the safety of sheltered doorways. We would like to hug our brother but are too shy with strangers present. In the kitchen's warmth, the young men begin to nod and doze, their heads dropping suddenly to their chests. They nudge each other with their feet in an attempt to keep awake. They will not stay and rest because they have come so far and tomorrow is Christmas Eve and stretches of mountains and water still lie between them and those they love. After they leave we pounce upon our brother physically and verbally. He laughs and shouts and lifts us over his head and swings us in his muscular arms. Yet in spite of his happiness he seems surprised at the appearance of his father whom he has not seen since March. My father merely smiles at him while my mother bites her lip.

Now that he is here there is a great flurry of activity. We have left everything we could until the time he might be with us. Eagerly I show him the fir tree on the hill which I have been watching for months and marvel at how easily he fells it and carries it down the hill. We fall over one another in the excitement of decoration.

He promises that on Christmas Eve he will take us to church in the sleigh behind the splendid horse that until his coming we are all afraid to handle. And on the afternoon of Christmas Eve he shoes the horse, lifting each hoof and rasping it fine and hammering the cherry-red horseshoes into shape upon the anvil. Later he drops them hissingly into the steaming tub of water. My father sits beside him on an overturned pail and tells him what to do. Sometimes we argue with our father, but our brother does everything he says.

That night, bundled in hay and voluminous coats, and with heated stones at our feet, we start upon our journey. Our parents and Kenneth remain at home but all the rest of us go. Before we leave we feed the cattle and sheep and even the pig all that they can possibly eat so that they will be contented on Christmas Eve. Our parents wave to us from the doorway. We go four miles across the mountain road. It is a primitive logging trail and there will be no cars or other vehicles upon it. At first the horse is wild with excitement and lack of exercise and my brother has to stand at the front of the sleigh and lean backwards on the reins. Later he settles down to a trot and still later to a walk as the mountain rises before him. We sing all the Christmas songs we know and watch for the rabbits and foxes scudding across the open patches of snow and listen to the drumming of partridge wings. We are never cold.

When we descend to the country church we tie the horse in a grove of trees where he will be sheltered and not frightened by the many cars. We put a blanket over him and give him oats.

At the church door the neighbours shake hands with my brother. "Hello, Neil," they say. "How is your father?"

"Oh," he says, just "Oh."

The church is very beautiful at night with its festooned branches and glowing candles and the booming, joyous sounds that come from the choir loft. We go through the service as if we are mesmerized.

On the way home, although the stones have cooled, we remain happy and warm. We listen to the creak of the leather harness and the hiss of runners on the snow and begin to think of the potentiality of presents. When we are about a mile from home the horse senses his destination and breaks into a trot and then into a confident lope. My brother lets him go and we move across the winter landscape like figures freed from a Christmas card. The snow from the horse's hooves falls about our heads like the whiteness of the stars.

After we have stabled the horse we talk with our parents and eat the meal our mother has prepared. And then I am sleepy and it is time for the younger children to be in bed. But tonight my father says to me, "We would like you to stay up with us a while," and so I stay quietly with the older members of my family.

When all is silent upstairs Neil brings in the cartons that contain his "clothes" and begins to open them. He unties the intricate knots quickly, their whorls falling away before his agile fingers. The boxes are filled with gifts neatly wrapped and bearing tags. The ones for my younger brothers say "from Santa Claus" but mine are not among them anymore, as I know with certainty they will never be again. Yet I am not so much surprised as touched by a pang of loss at being here on the adult side of the world. It is as if I have suddenly moved into another room and heard a door click lastingly behind me. I am jabbed by my own small wound.

But then I look at those before me. I look at my parents drawn together before the Christmas tree. My mother has her hand upon my father's shoulder and he is holding his ever-present handkerchief. I look at my sisters who have crossed this threshold ahead of me and now each day journey farther from the lives they knew as girls. I look at my magic older brother who has come to us this Christmas from half a continent away, bringing everything he has and is. All of them are captured in the tableau of their care.

"Every man moves on," says my father quietly, and I think he speaks of Santa Claus, "but there is no need to grieve. He leaves good things behind."

Second Spring

IT WAS THE summer after the seventh grade that saw me truly smitten with the calf club wish. It was not, of course, a really dazzlingly new idea because, living on a farm, I had always been surrounded by numerous animals. Not a day went by without touching them and the insistence of their presence affected the living of my life and the lives of the other members of my family in very real and tangible ways. Their closeness and the manner of their closeness varied with the time of seasons.

In the winter when they were less plentiful, they crowded together in the shared and dense confinement of their stables; stamping their hooves on the manure-strong planking and tossing their impatient heads and uttering the sounds of their different species. If you ventured into the silent barn at night the wave of their communal warmth rolled out to meet you at the creaking, opened door and the sound of the different rhythms of their breathing rose and fell in the softened darkness. If the flashlight was flicked on, or the carried lantern raised, the luminous eyes of those who were awakened glowed from their stalls and across their mangers, and then various sounds seemed to respond to the presence of the light; the creak of the wooden stanchion posts rubbed by the necks of restless cattle, the murmured grunts of half-asleep pigs, the nickering snorts of horses, the zing of suddenly tightened rope or leather, the jangle of moving halter chains.

By March conditions were even more overcrowded as the females grew awkward and ponderous with the weight of their unborn young. When they lay down in their expanded heaviness the ripples of movement from deep within their wombs were visible against the drum-tight skin of their extended sides. The promise of the future lay warm and heavy within their deep, dark bodies.

Inside the winter house the dogs and cats lay like scattered rugs beneath the kitchen couches and under dining tables or stretched at length behind the wood-filled stoves. At night my dog Laddie lay across my feet; a warm and living comforter whose heartbeat could be felt through the fabric of the bedclothes. His wet, cold nose was covered by his paws.

By the end of March the birth cycle would begin and would extend sometimes deep into June. First the sheep, then some cattle and later the pigs and finally the wobbly foals with their long, ungainly legs. There would be chickens and kittens and puppies with at-first-unopened eyes. The number of animals would double or almost triple within the allotted weeks and there would be a flurry of activity surrounding the new arrivals and the rapidity of their growth. New pens would be constructed and, amidst squeals of protest, there would be separations, weanings and brandings and the pulling of teeth and the flashing of knives used for the cutting of testicles, the docking of tails and the notching of ears. They would spill out then, according to their kind, to the larger yards and fields or the mountain-high pastures washed by the blue-white sea.

By July first, which always seemed unbelievably soon, the haying season which would ensure their winter's survival would begin. During the summer months while the animals grew sleek and fat and haughty, we, their human owners, would grow thin and burned and irritable; rising often before sunrise and working sometimes until after dark. Only the work horses seemed to share in our drudgery and weight loss; the burns from their collars and the chafings caused by their rubbing traces corresponding to the blisters and calluses upon our hands. Sometimes at night we would rub ourselves with diluted horse liniment to alleviate the sprains and bruises which we accumulated during the day.

Throughout this season, as I said, the animals of summer grew strong and free. Only the milk cows were brought to the barn twice daily for their milking and even they seemed to take on an air of independence that bordered close to arrogance. The others grazed openly and heedlessly through the long days of their summer vacation. From the tops of our hay wagons we could see them, especially on the hottest days, lying on the sandy beaches which separated their pastures from the sea or dangerously close to the rocky edge of the sea cliffs fall. It was always cooler near the sea and there was always a slight breeze and they were not bothered there by the flies that tormented inland animals. Throughout the working days of summer we spent little time ourselves beside or within the turquoise sea.

As the summer progressed and as the season's young became more independent, the mature animals would yearn again to be sexually active. They would demonstrate their needs in various ways, again depending on their species and their sex, and they would continue to do so until they were fulfilled. We, as the humans who depended on them as they did on us, would frequently and of necessity interfere with their needs and desires. We would tether the lusty and often ill-tempered rams to iron stakes driven deep into the earth or isolate them in all-male pens where they frequently took out their frustrations by battering their thick-boned skulls against each other. We would keep them from the ewes until late in the fall, knowing that early matings resulted in the birth of winter lambs who stood little chance of surviving the bitter coldness of the season of their birth. We would keep the young heifers from the heavy bulls, knowing that they were often injured and sometimes permanently maimed in their first sexual encounters and knowing also that even if they did survive the breeding, great difficulty awaited them in such youthful pregnancies and that often they would die attempting to give birth. Another year would make a great difference to them as well as to us. In the same manner we would discourage nesting and maternal hens from bringing forth autumnal chickens who would not be matured enough to meet the demands of cold, rain-lashed November and the harsher months to follow. Like highly protective parents we would hover over such lives, hoping that our attempts at control would result in what was "best" for all. This is for your own good, we would think, as well as for ours, although we would never articulate it in such a manner.

In the fall we would reduce the population that had so flourished through the long, hot summer days. As it had doubled or tripled in the spring, it was reduced by similar numbers in the fall, and reduced in a variety of ways. Livestock buyers came, sometimes walking to the pastures to view their intended victims, offering prices, quoting possibilities, leaving and returning. All of the male lambs would go, and most of the females except a select few singled out to continue the reproductive cycle. When they left, they would be strong and rambunctious, unlike their earlier wobbly-legged selves. They would crowd against one another and jostle as they were ushered up the ramps of the waiting trucks and sometimes they would attempt to leap over the slatted sides of their new confinement. We would hear their indignant bleatings as the trucks took them permanently from the single environment of their one and only summer. Sounds of angered indignation tinged with the very real sound of fear. Later the cheques we had exchanged them for would come and we, in our turn, would enter a phase of rejuvenation and hopeful, though temporary, self-confidence.

Sometimes, depending on different factors, it would be more profitable to butcher animals and sell them locally than to trust to the simpler yet more bureaucratic expedient of the truck or train which would take them to more distant killing stations. There was always butchering in the late fall to supply meat for ourselves and our urban relatives, but in some years there would be more than in others. It would always be a melancholy time then, especially if there was a lot of it. The night before we would lay out the ceremonial clothes of death, splattered with bloodstains and bearing the distinctive odour which could never be fully washed away. We would sit on chairs in the kitchen, sharpening the various knives and testing the keenness of the blades with the balls of our callused thumbs. We would pay attention to the weather and nearly always kill according to the phases of the moon. From the barn we could hear the protesting moans of the unknowing and condemned animals. Unlike condemned prisoners, they would receive neither food nor water before their executions. This was to reduce the bulk of their weight and their body fluids for the day that was to follow; so that their weight, which would so soon become dead, would be less ponderous and easier to handle.

On the day of the actual butchering we would rise early so that we would get a good start. In the late fall the days would be short and since we would normally work by natural light, adjustments would have to be made. The animal would be taken to that part of the barn called the threshing floor and stationed beneath the chain pulleys which would soon be used to elevate its carcass. If it were a huge animal, it would be shot. Sometimes we would draw lines on its trusting head with a crayon, from behind each ear and across its forehead. Generally the point of intersection would be the marksman's target —

almost a literal bull's-eye. If the animal were less huge, it would be merely hit between the eyes by a sledgehammer or the blunt side of an axe wielded by the strongest man. Even as its front legs buckled and its eyes glazed, the knife used for the severing of the jugular would be passed handle-first to the waiting hands which had tossed aside the sledgehammer or axe – much as the nurse might pass the scalpel. If done well, it would take but ten or twelve seconds to change life into death. The pigs were always the hardest to kill because their skulls slanted backwards and were more difficult to strike than the flattened foreheads of others. As the blood gushed from the slashed throats, we would gather it in pans so that it might later be used for blood puddings – *maragan,* they were called in Gaelic. One person would hold the pan beneath the neck of the fallen animal while another would raise and steady the convulsing and partly severed head so that the blood would be pumped into the pan and not wasted on the barn-planked floor. Later we would take the hind legs and cut the flesh between the hocks and the main tendons and insert a horizontal stick. To this stick we would fasten the now-descended chain pulleys and we would raise the animal by its widespread legs even as we skinned and disembowelled it. Sometimes the flesh would continue to twitch for a long time after the actual death and even after the hide had been removed. The contents of the body would generally spill into a huge washtub and we would sort them out in their steaming warmth with bloodied slippery hands. We would save at least the heart and the liver and the stomach and the strips of marbled fat; sometimes other portions as well. And if there was time, our father would point out and explain the functions of the mysterious and until-now invisible internal organs. "This is the bladder, and this is the spleen and this is the large intestine. This is the windpipe. These are the lungs. This is the passage that the seed follows from the testicles to the end of the penis." We would listen and watch intently, like those involved in a formal autopsy or like intense medical students about their still cadaver.

Often there would be surprises. Sometimes shingle nails or fence staples or bits of twisted wire would be found imbedded in the stomach, and one time the neck of a beer bottle was found completely surrounded by a strange almost translucent knob of gristle. It seemed to glow like a huge, obscene pearl. We remembered then how more than a year ago the cow had stood for days unable to eat or give milk and for a while barely able to walk. We had no way of knowing then how the sharp-edged amber glass she had carelessly swallowed in her grazing cut into her stomach's lining, and we did not know when the gristle began to surround it and isolate it, thus allowing her to move and function once again. Another time we found an unborn calf within the womb of a young cow we had considered sterile. We had tried various matings and solutions but she had always failed to conceive. In her fourth year of life her sterility became a luxury we could not afford. "We cannot take her through another winter like that," was the verdict. "She will have to be fattened and killed." When found within the womb of the slaughtered mother, the embryonic calf continued to move for a brief and borrowed time. Its delicate limbs had begun to form and were folded compactly back upon themselves while its eyes seemed large and luminous. Its ears were exquisite and fragile and flatly pressed like the memory of ferns found deep within the darkened earth. No one knew who had fathered the calf, although the time could be roughly estimated. What we had wanted we had found achieved, when it was ironically too late to save the life of either.

Such scenes of selling and butchering would repeat themselves until a rough balance between livestock and available hay was achieved. In dry seasons when the hay crop was less lush there would have to be a corresponding reduction in animal numbers. In years that were more bountiful we could afford to winter individuals who would not have survived the more rigorous selectivity of leaner years. The selection of those who would remain and those who would "go" was always a tight and careful process. Like shrewd and thoughtful managers of athletic teams preparing their lists of protected players, we would go over the strengths and weaknesses of each individual. Age was always a factor, as was general strength; fertility, as I mentioned, another and sometimes even what might be called "personality." Animals who were particularly ill-tempered or high-strung or who had developed bad habits, like leaping fences or raiding summer vegetable gardens, received thoughtful scrutiny as the deadline approached. And as always, if the troublesome individuals had outstanding positive traits, they would be given additional leeway and allowed to make it for another year. Sheep who produced "weighty" lambs or a high proportion of twins were forgiven balancing weaknesses and the cows who were the leading milk producers were generally grudgingly indulged, regardless of how unpleasant they actually might be. They were often the "stars" on not overly strong teams and were catered to accordingly.

I say all of this now so that you might understand the environment in which the calf club wish was born, and also so that you might see the situation in which it existed for a while – wobbly and uncertain but grounded in a kind of realism similar to the animals and the people who were its basic source.

The idea itself, however, came from a new person in our midst. In the late winter and early spring of the seventh grade a new and dynamic agricultural representative began to visit our two-room school. He was young and athletic and brimming with vigour. He was one year away from the completion of his degree and had interrupted his formal studies for a year of "in-the-field" practical experience; and we were to be part of his field. He was almost contagious. We had always had visits from agricultural representatives but they were for the most part men who were older and gave the impression of wishing they were somewhere else. One used to wear a suede jacket and a pair of grey trousers covered with cigarette ashes and other interesting stains. He would sit at the desk in the front of the room and ask if there were any questions. There would seldom be any, so he would ask one: "Well, then what will we talk about?" Then he would look out the window rather longingly, as would we, hoping for, if not a discussion topic, a sort of mutual deliverance. Another used to show slides of "common North American weeds." He seemed to come later in the year, in May or June, and always in the afternoon. Each slide bore the name of the weed which was illustrated, and he would read the label aloud to us in a ritual which we came to call weed parade. "Common Ragwort," he would say, or "Scottish Thistle" or "Wild Onion" or "Broadleaved Dock." He would always glance surreptitiously at his watch and drink from a thermos bottle of coffee laced with whiskey. In the drowsy hot afternoons as weed followed weed and their names became more slurred and the vapours from the whiskied coffee rose around us, we would find it almost impossible to stay awake. But our new man changed all that.

First he said that in addition to our present vegetable garden clubs we should start a calf club. He had been doing research, he said, and all we needed was a minimum of ten heifer calves produced by a pure-bred sire. These would be born the following spring so it was not too early to begin thinking of their conception. The mothers could be "any cow of high quality." Such quality would hopefully be transferred to her daughter. We would need a paper signed by the keeper of the pure-bred sire, indicating the breeding date and the hopeful conception of the desired calf. We were to check our cattle at home and speak with our parents. We were interested in dairy cattle so we should not select a beef-type mother. Neither should we "cross" breeds if we could help it. We should not breed a cow with heavy Holstein characteristics to an Ayrshire bull, for example, because the breed characteristics would become confused. His research had shown that the predominant strain in the area was Ayrshire and there were two Ayrshire bulls approximately ten miles apart and subsidized by the Department of Agriculture. These bulls, he said, were not being "utilized to their full potential." We copied it all down in our scribblers to refer to at a later time.

On our way home I considered all the cattle that we owned, thinking of their backgrounds and their breeding and when they were due to give birth that spring. I was already a year ahead of myself in searching for my candidate for mother of the year. I settled mentally on a large and consistently gentle cow whom we called Morag. She was basically white with cherry-red markings and long and sweeping elegant Ayrshire horns. She possessed almost all of the "high-quality" requirements which had been mentioned and she would deliver her current "ordinary" calf quite early in the spring. She had always conceived quickly and easily following the births of her other calves, and I could not believe my good fortune.

When I entered our house my father was fixing harness in the kitchen. He was not in a good mood, I realized, but I was so enthusiastic that I told him all about the new agricultural representative and our potential calf club, falling over my words in my excitement.

"Oh," he said with something like vague annoyance, "I've heard all that before. Those agricultural representatives are all the same. They just talk and talk and talk and never do anything. They come in their fancy cars in the middle of the haying season and expect you to drop everything and talk to them. Almost everything they say is common sense anyway: 'Plant early and you will harvest early.' 'Rotate your crops.' 'Use lime.' 'Heavy rainfall results in a high yield.' 'Turkeys are needed for the Thanksgiving market.' Who doesn't know that? What they say is all baloney."

"Well," I said, thinking I had best keep on. "It would just be one cow. I was thinking of Morag after her calf is born. There is a pure-bred Agricultural Society bull at MacDougall's five miles away. We could breed her there in the summer."

"Not me," he said. "I'm not dragging any more cows on the end of a rope to one of those bulls. I kept one of those Agricultural Society bulls here myself about fifteen years ago. More trouble than he was worth. Took up too much space in the barn. Had to haul feed and water to him all the time because he was too dangerous to let out. Then if he didn't get exercise he wouldn't breed properly. And people always came with cows at the damndest times. Seven o'clock on Sunday morning. Anytime there was a wedding or a funeral. Anytime you were leaving the house you'd be sure to meet someone with a cow and have to go back in and change your clothes and go handle the bull for them. Bull got so he wouldn't let anyone else around him but me, so I could never leave the house. People would come with their cows and if I weren't home they'd complain. Not that they didn't have a right to, I suppose."

He began to gather up his harness from the floor in preparation for the evening chores. I felt that perhaps I should point out that all of our best cattle were still descendants of that long-departed bull but it somehow did not seem a good day for that kind of logic. After he had gone to the barn, my mother said: "He is not having a good day but you realize he did not say 'No.' Ask him something definite and volunteer to do the work yourself. He is getting tired. You know that if he gives you his word, he will always keep it."

It was true. Whatever uneven moods my father was prone to, he possessed a memory which did not permit him to forget anything and he was always true to his word. In retrospect, it does not seem that we were certain of many things, dwelling in the realm of fluctuating weather and fickle seasons and aggressive insects and indifferent soil; but of those traits we were sure, and we clung to them as the uneasy swimmer to his certain log.

In the barn it was growing dark. My father moved about the animals with a tired familiarity, leaning against them, pushing them with his shoulder as he moved towards their mangers, talking to them in a sort of abbreviated private language, pulling manure with his fork from beneath them, tightening their halter chains, distributing their feed so that it was within their reach.

"Okay," he said before I had time to speak. "I didn't say you couldn't, just that I wouldn't. If you raise the fee, you can have the cow."

It was, it seemed, fair enough.

The fee was probably part of the reason we had stopped using the Agricultural Society bull in the first place. Another was that it took valuable time in a period before the widespread use of trucks and artificial insemination. "He," the bull, had gone too far away and it was no longer considered worth it. It was expensive, as I mentioned, and there was also a feeling that paying money for the simple breeding act was a bit too much – as if it were somehow unnatural, a kind of perversion or animal prostitution in which we cared not to be involved; as if there were an uneasy idea that no one should have to "pay for it." There was also the shrewd and pragmatic observation that after a few years of such selective breeding most cattle already contained "good" if not exactly royal blood and further exalted matings were perhaps a waste of time. It was probably a reaction to such spreading ideas that the agricultural representative had come among us in the first place to plant the seeds of the calf club wish.

In any case, I had achieved the first step. Before the birth of Morag's present calf, I had already willed her pregnant once again. I entered my name with the agricultural representative and told my fellow schoolmates that I would "go." The snow had not yet melted, nor had the wild ducks flown north, nor had the first spring lambs and early kittens yet been born, but I was already well into not only this spring but the next as well.

After the birth of Morag's "ordinary" calf, there followed the long period of waiting. If she were to deliver the magic calf by early next spring, she would have to conceive in the middle of summer. It took nine months from conception to birth – "just like people," as we used to say. "Cattle are the only animals that take the same length of time."

As the spring passed and the early summer approached, the hectic pace of our lives increased. School drew to a close and during the last few weeks we attended it irregularly. We were needed at home and whatever we had learned during the year was already in our past. Feverish preparations for the approaching haying season began: the repairing of machinery, the sending away for parts, improvements to the barn and also a myriad of other activities involving gardening, canning and the making of cheese. The short intense summer was upon us and we had no time to lose.

Meanwhile the animals grew sleek and fat and were distant from us most of the time as we prepared to gather in their winter sustenance. In the early weeks of July we began our haying in earnest; cutting the most mature fields and leaving them to dry, then raking and finally pitching onto the wagons, then driving into the barn and pitching off and returning again and then again. Always threatened by broken harness and non-functioning machinery and always fearful of the sudden spectre of rain.

On the evening of the fourteenth of July I noticed the signs in Morag when I was bringing the milk cows home from their pasture by the sea. She was coming into her breeding cycle and it caused a restlessness and tension not only within herself but among the other cattle as well. It was late in the evening when I first noticed it and there was nothing I could do that day. That night the radio told us of the approaching rain squalls which were to hit on the following day.

"Goddamn it," said my father, "and us with all that hay out."

We had just recently cut a new field so much of it was still undried. In the morning we were up at five, moving feverishly about our tasks, racing against the weather. At the morning milking Morag's situation was truly obvious, although my father did not notice. He was not around the cattle much but busy harnessing the horses and shouting directions to animals and people alike. The clouds were already bunching, although they still seemed far enough away, hanging over the ocean and visible from a distance.

"Hurry up," he said, coming into the barn where I was milking the cows. "It's going to rain. We haven't got all day."

"I think we should keep Morag in the barn today," I stammered quickly, fearful lest he should get away before I broached the subject.

"What for?" he asked and I could see that he was so harried and preoccupied that he had given my words but little thought.

"She's in heat," I said. "She began last night."

For a moment his eyes seemed to cloud over with non-comprehension, but then they cleared and became filled almost with panic, as he understood the significance of my words. It was as if he were trapped by his memory and his word. Trapped by them at this, his busiest time.

"But there is no time today," he sputtered. "We have other things to do than just worry about this one goddamn cow."

"Okay," I said. "We will just keep her in and see what the day brings. I didn't say I wanted to go with her now."

"Okay," he said, as if he were relieved of an earlier capricious promise. "Take the others down to the shore. We have to get going."

What the day brought was a forenoon of furious activity. First we raked the driest hay and then followed with the groaning wagons. The sun shone erratically but the air was so humid that little actual drying took place. At times the clouds blotted out the sun and once we could actually see the rain falling out to sea, although it had not yet started to fall upon the land. All morning as we raced about, raising new blisters upon the calluses already formed on our hands, Morag moaned and bawled her passion from the barn. When we came in with the loaded wagons, we could hear her threshing about in the frustration of her captivity and her desire.

I would have liked to bring her a pail of water to ease her thirst, although I knew that was not what she really wanted – but there was no time even for that. On one or two occasions I thought I heard an answering call from what seemed like a great distance but I could not really be sure. She was safe in the barn anyway, I thought. Safe for me, if not satisfied for herself. Our work intensified, as did the weather which surrounded us.

When the storm finally broke, it announced itself first in two thunderous cracks and a jagged scar of lightning across the sky and then the rain seemed to hurl itself down as if pressurized forth from the hanging, laden clouds. Everything and everyone became immediately drenched and to save even the half-loaded wagon of imperfectly dried hay we had to shout to the horses and swing the reins over their already steaming backs. They broke into a gallop then, jolting the wagon behind them until they careened into the still, dignified safety of the waiting barn. Within five minutes it was obvious that the day's haying was over and that at a future time we would have to begin again with what was now being so thoroughly soaked. But by then the hay would not be the same but only of the second grade.

The rain poured down all afternoon; rivulets streamed down the windows and the sides of the buildings and cascaded down the laneways, pushing erratic, insistent trenches through the softened earth. Nothing but the water seemed to move. The ocean was still and we were still ourselves after all our desperate activity. Even Morag's passion seemed to lull as if she were cooled and covered by the soothing of the rain. It was late that evening before I could venture down to the shore to bring the milk cows home, and by the next morning Morag was ravenously hungry but otherwise in no way outwardly exceptional. The hope for the mid-April calf was gone and would not come again.

For two days it was overcast and there were sporadic showers and the cut and sodden hay began gradually to turn black. On the third day it cleared in the afternoon and by the fourth day the sun shone again and we began to pick up where we had left off prior to the storm. We did not pick up at the same place, for part of our crop was gone or greatly deteriorated. I set my sights on the approximate three-week future and rationalized that a mid-May calf would, after all, not really be so bad.

I was ready in August because I had mentally noted the earlier date. We were still at our haying, although many of the fields had now been cleared. We were all thinner and more irritable and beset by various nagging injuries which bore witness to the activities of our past days and weeks. A thumbnail torn off by a running rope, a back spasm caused by lifting too heavy a pitch, a swollen jaw caused by the unexpected disturbance of a wasp's nest within the deepened grass, a purplish plate-sized bruise on the thigh caused by the kick of a horse irritated by flies.

When I recognized the August signs in Morag, it was in the morning and the day promised to be clear and hot. We were on the home stretch of our summer's haying and things were not as desperate as they had been in the earlier month. I mentioned the situation to my father and he said that I should keep Morag in the barn that day. That evening, after we had done a reasonable day's work, he said, I could be free to go on my five-mile journey. All day as we worked I was intent on my future mission. I was actually a bit afraid as the time drew closer, contemplating the twists and turns of the road I must go, and realizing even then how erratic it might be. From the barn Morag moaned and bawled, her voice sounding like the theme music for the day's production. The answer seemed to come from far away.

In the evening after the other milk cows were stabled, I placed a halter on Morag's head, looped an additional length of rope around her sweeping horns and prepared to set off.

"Don't wrap the rope too tightly around your hand," said my father, "because if she bolts she might pull your shoulder out of its socket." He was on his way to finish the last hay load of the evening.

"Okay," I said, doubling the rope within my hand.

The five-mile journey was a narrow dirt road which followed the erratic indentations of the sea. It was apparently the original path followed by the first settlers in the 1770s when they walked along the shore on their way to their new lands. Now it was almost a private road, rarely used by any automotive traffic because it was so narrow and so dangerous, but used by people on missions such as mine, by people on foot, or those on horseback; sometimes by lovers, sometimes by drunkards or a variety of others who did not appreciate detection. At times it clung to the cliffs and in certain places the edges of it had crumbled and fallen down into the sea some two hundred feet below.

As we began the journey, Morag moved rapidly and I was forced to run to keep by her side. I could feel the strength of her head and shoulders almost surging back along the rope like a current and thought uneasily that if she were to lunge I would not be able to control her. Contrary to what I had been told, I wrapped the rope around my hand, figuring that if she had to drag me, she at least would not escape. We covered the first mile rapidly and both of us were breathing heavily. She will soon tire, I thought, and then she will be easier to handle.

After the first mile the road began to climb steeply and the small rocks rolled beneath our feet but still she did not seem to slacken much.

In one way this is good, I thought. At least we are getting there in a hurry.

I had had an earlier vision of her standing stubbornly in the middle of the road while I tried in vain to urge her on. This was obviously not going to be the case – at least not for the first two miles. After the climb the road passed through a sort of upland plateau for perhaps three hundred yards and then became a series of hairpin turns. Suddenly and unexpectedly it dipped and rose and twisted in such a manner as to make it impossible to see what was ahead. It was in the middle of the second turn that we saw him or perhaps heard him first. There was a low rumble in his throat which he continually repeated as he approached us coming down the hill.

The hill at this spot rose from the cliff edge of the sea which was on our right and ascended steeply before levelling off into another plateau. On that plateau I could now see a herd of cattle in the distance and he was coming from them and rapidly bearing down on us. He weighed perhaps a ton, with immense shoulders and an enormous chest. He was mostly white but his head and neck were a brindled grey which shaded at times almost into blue. He carried his head low as he moved and moaned towards us with strands of bead-like saliva falling from his lower jaw. His horns were thick and yellowed and spiralled downward and outward like those of a mountain sheep. No formal heritage was visible in the way he looked or the way he moved, and there was nothing like him in any book entitled *Standard Breeds of Cattle*.

He was approaching quickly now, coming down the hill towards us, the grade of the hill seeming to give him added momentum. He was walking very rapidly and determinedly with that low moaning rumble in his throat, but he was not running. He was not running at all like those bulls run in the jokes about bulls after cows. None of us, I knew, were in any joke. At the base of the hill beside the road there was a rail fence which formed a separation but I could see that the rails and the posts were rotten and that they represented perhaps more the idea of a fence than the fact of one. I thought that with his size and speed and the downward grade of the hill he would perhaps jump over it, but instead he merely walked through it as if it did not exist at all. The whole section of the fence parted to his progress like the furrow before the breaking plough or the water before the ongoing ship. The edges of the rotted, broken rails seemed to cling to his flanks as he passed through their destruction but they had no effect upon his movement. He continued to bear down upon us rapidly but also unhurriedly, as if he were very certain of everything and very much in control.

In romantic retrospect, I see myself sometimes as one of those "guides" in the Gothic novels, attempting to guard my tremulous female figure from the lascivious, slobbering male who, in the fulfilling of his desires, will cause irrevocable pain. Or by another extension the "concerned father" who will do almost anything to keep his vulnerable daughter from the one he knows to be not right for her. Defence against the figure "with but one thing on his mind."

But in the reality of that evening's dusty road, she swung her head towards him with swift and arching strength. Her sweeping horns seemed almost to whistle through the air and she lifted me, with the rope wrapped tightly around my hand, completely off my feet. As if I were some slight and ridiculous irritant she could no longer tolerate. She swung my body almost into his looming head and I could see, as under a microscope, the dark and deepened liquid of his eyes, the gnarled, yellow rings at the base of his horns, his grey-blue jowls and the strings of beaded saliva trailing from his jaw. I could smell the sweet, heavy hotness of his grass-filled breath as their muzzles touched, and for an instant I thought I might lose my own life if either horned head should swing in the wrong direction. Then with a moan he swung behind her and reared up massively, his heavy shoulders silhouetted and rising into the evening sun which was settling now to the waiting sea. It seemed in that moment as if Morag were approaching her answer even as I was to be denied mine.

"Is that what you want?" came a voice near at hand.

"No," I said or perhaps sobbed, "no," almost before noticing where the voice came from.

"Christ," he said, sliding from the back of the horse almost in one motion.

He too had come upon us suddenly and unexpectedly around the hairpin turn. He was apparently coming from the village, judging from the two rum bottles which protruded from his faded blue overalls, and it seemed he had not been hurrying because the huge, black horse which immediately began to crop the roadside grass showed no signs of perspiration. He was an old man then, deep into his seventies, and was my grandfather's cousin and therefore also mine. He was a tremendously big man and had lived the kind of reckless life that big men sometimes lead in such communities – perhaps because there was often no one to stop them from doing almost anything they wanted. He was to die at a future time, late at night and in mysterious darkness, falling or pushed from the rickety balcony outside a bootlegger's second-storey door. His neck was broken when he was discovered and his money gone and someone had cut the reins of his black horse and its companion as they stood hitched to the steel-wheeled wagon and waiting as on so many other nights. They had galloped home then, wildly through the night, the sparks flashing from the steel of their shoes as they swung the wagon behind them, lifting it off its wheels in the tightest turns and suspending it for seconds over the cliff's edge and above the darkened sea. The people who lived along the road had been awakened by the sound of the rushing horses and had recognized them from the sure-footed terror of their hoofbeats in the same manner that their descendants now recognize the individual motor sounds of different cars. They had heard the sounds before and did not know that on this occasion the black horses were careening through the night, driverless and without a human guide.

When the horses arrived home they were covered with froth, the muscles of their shoulders and flanks trembled and twitched and their eyes were glassy and wild. The people of the house came out then and with lanterns and flashlights began to retrace the journey of the wagon, seeking to find him in the roadside ditch or over the cliff's edge on the boulders touched by the sea, or even perhaps lying sprawled in the middle of the road. But they did not find him all that night and in the morning someone brought the official, final news. They noticed then that the reins had been cut and wondered why they had not noticed it before.

But that is ahead of my story. For at that meeting on the narrow road and in the presence of the bull, we did not know what future was in store for any of us. Our present seemed too real.

In memory, now, he moved with tremendous speed, although he did not seem to hurry and the illusion was probably due to the length of his legs and the amount of ground he covered in a single step. Without breaking stride, he bent down and his right hand scooped up a large rock which lay by the roadside. It seemed almost the size of a bowling ball yet he carried it easily and lightly in his gigantic hand. As he approached the rearing, lunging bull, he extended his left hand up and forward until it grasped one of the mountain sheep horns and then in one fluid arc of motion and follow-through, he brought the rocky boulder down between the bull's concentrated, widespread eyes. The thud of the rock on skull was like the sound on the butchering days and the bull toppled sideways and to his knees. His eyes, drained of their passion, rolled glassily upwards in their sockets, and two thin streams of saliva now green from regurgitated grass trickled from his nostrils and back into his sagging mouth. His penis, still dripping fluid, collapsed limply within its sheath. His day's breeding or attempted breeding was over.

"Did he get it in?" he said, wiping his hand on his overalls and then reaching for one of the rum bottles.

"I don't know," I said. "I couldn't see."

"If he got it in," he said, "you never can be sure. What are you doing here anyway apart from trying to get yourself killed?"

Briefly and disjointedly I stammered out the nature of my mission.

"Well," he said, "you may as well keep going. I'll go with you partway if you want. Here, you jump on the horse."

Easily and with the same arm he had used for the rock, he lifted me up to the back of the horse and then passed me the reins. He took Morag's rope in his hand and almost automatically she began to move in step with him while I followed behind on the horse. I looked back once at the bull and he was still kneeling and partially lying by the roadside where he had been struck down. His head seemed to loll to one side.

After we had negotiated the remainder of the hairpin turns and had travelled perhaps a mile, he stopped and passed Morag's rope towards me. I dismounted from the horse, exchanging the reins for the proffered rope.

"You should be all right now," he said. "Perhaps you should go back by the other road."

Taking a deep pull from one of his rum bottles, he mounted the black horse and turned him in the direction of his original homeward journey.

Morag and I continued on our way more quietly and more slowly than when we had set out. When we entered the laneway to the MacDougall yard, the sun was almost setting and I could see that they were hurrying to get their last load of hay into the barn before darkness. Mr. MacDougall was on top of the hay wagon, organizing the pitches tossed up by the others, and he was not awfully glad to see us.

"Jesus H. Christ, another goddamn cow," he said, driving his fork deep into the hay before him. I was reminded of my father's earlier remarks.

Nevertheless, he climbed down from the wagon and his place was taken by one of his sons. On the way to the barn, I told him what had happened.

"Did he get it in?" he asked.

"I don't know," I said, "I couldn't see."

"He probably didn't," he said, "if it happened as fast as you say. Perhaps he didn't reach her. Sometimes it takes them a while to get set. Anyway, we'll just have to see."

I stood in the dusky yard, clutching Morag's rope and waiting for the cherry-red and white bull with all the proper characteristics to come moaning forth, guided by a long wooden staff snapped into the ring of his nose. The breeding was almost leisurely and seemed thorough.

"Well, this one is sure as hell in," said MacDougall appreciatively. "No doubt about that. It should be all right."

After the bull was returned to his barn, I paid MacDougall the fee and he went into his house and then returned with a scribbler from which he tore a page. On it he wrote the date and Morag's ownership and the fact that the breeding had occurred. He squinted his eyes in the dusky gloom and his hands were heavy and thick and unaccustomed to holding the stubby, yellow pencil. The funky odour of the bull's perspiration and semen still hung about his hands and about the man himself.

On the return we took a more travelled route and I was afraid as the darkness descended that we might be hit by a passing car or truck, but there was little traffic and we walked steadily and briskly. Although the route was longer, the return journey seemed much shorter than the outgoing one, the way return journeys often do. It was totally dark when we entered our own yard and my father was in the barn where he seemed to be waiting.

"How did you get along?" he asked.

Again, I stated my story.

"Do you think he got it in?" he asked.

"I don't know," I said.

I was so exhausted I could hardly stand. My father took Morag's rope from me and led her into the barn. I went into the house and to bed without eating any supper. The mark from Morag's rope still burned and circled redly about my hand and wrist.

During the weeks that followed I played and replayed the events of the day within the privacy of my mind. I half hoped she had not conceived so that we could perhaps start over again; but I knew that if she had not, valuable time would already be lost and a September mating would at best produce a summer calf instead of a spring one; and that would perhaps be too late for the calf club's organization. When the September dates came, I watched Morag anxiously but there were no signs. She grazed contentedly and lay in the sun by the sea and walked home placidly to be milked. She seemed at ease with everything.

We went into September seriously then with a new round of activities: grain crops had to be harvested and preparations began for the digging of potatoes. School reopened and I was in the eighth grade. There were various fall fairs and exhibitions and our agricultural representative was everywhere. The first truckload of lambs was hauled away, bleating in the autumn sun, and the vines and tendrils of the vegetable gardens turned to russet and then to darker brown.

In October Morag was still quiet and calm when the serious butchering and selling began, and by Halloween when the first snow fell she and the other animals entered the stables for their winter confinement.

All winter I watched her anxiously and nervously, almost as

if I were the young expectant father. When she began to grow heavier I moved her to a special stall so she might have more room, and sometimes I would place my hands and arms around her expanded girth, hoping I might feel life. When first I felt it, we were already out of the coldest depth of winter and into the erratic, gale-filled month of March. The calf became even more real then, as I lead her through my mind in various elegant postures and positions.

Spring came early that year and although the nights remained cold, during the days the sun shone warmly down upon our backs as we went about repairing fences and replacing sluices and generally rectifying the ravages of winter. By May first the cattle were out during the day busily seeking the first adventurous blades of grass. During the first week the older more mature animals still sought the relative warmth of the stable at night while the younger ones seemed quite willing to give up warmth for the advantages of freedom. I was torn between Morag's giving birth outside where there would be less chance of infection but possible dangers from the cold or keeping her inside where her surroundings would be warmer but more constricted and less sanitary. She was now so heavy that she seemed almost to fall when she lay down and she had great difficulty in getting up.

In the late afternoon of the tenth of May when I went down to the shore for the cows I could not see Morag among them and I knew then that her time had come, apart from any decision that might be mine. I searched for half an hour, knowing that she would not give birth near the sea which was still dotted with the winter's ice floes and the source of chilling winds, so I began to criss-cross the wooded hollows and the inland sheltered gatherings of spruce. Finally I found her heavy tracks deep in the wet spring earth. They were already nearly filled with water, indicating that she had passed a considerable time before. I followed them across a small stream which trickled from a marsh and then around the edge of the marsh itself and then up a steep incline and finally to the edge of a considerable grove of spruce and fir.

The trees of the grove were closely crowded together. Parting the branches and still following the heavy tracks in the brown needled floor, I came suddenly into a small clearing which was almost like a room. The edges of it were bordered by wild brambles which had not yet begun to bud and there were also several older heavier trees which had been uprooted and toppled by the winter winds and now lay like heavy barriers along the wooded perimeter. There seemed no way out of it except through the entranceway that we had used. Morag was lying on her side when I entered. She was already greatly dilated and the mucus discharge had begun. She struggled to her feet when I entered and swung her horns towards me and for a moment I was afraid that she might charge even as the unborn calf began to protrude. But then she became calmer and after pacing several preparatory circles she flopped heavily down upon her side once more.

As in all births, it seemed surprisingly fast once it actually began. After all the months of our waiting, it seemed to take no time at all.

His shoulders were heavy and thick and his chest was large. He was mostly white but his head and neck were a brindled grey that shaded at times almost into blue. No formal heritage was visible in the way he looked and there was nothing like him in any book entitled *Standard Breeds of Cattle*. Morag rose and turned to lick the mucus from his nostrils and nudged him with her nose. Almost immediately he tried to struggle to his feet, clothed in the shimmering curtains of placenta which hung transparently from about his newborn frame.

He tottered and fell and tottered and fell but then seemed to gain control of his wobbly legs even as his mother's nose pushed him firmly but gently towards his first nursing. They seemed very glad to see each other, and if disappointment was mine it obviously was not shared by them.

The calf club wish ended there in the tiny groved room on the tenth of May when the eighth grade was not yet completed.

I do not think I had to work as hard that summer. Perhaps it was just that the weather was better. Or that I was older. Or that my parents were doing more than I realized. Perhaps all of them together. Anyway, there seemed to be more free time, and that was the summer I flung myself into baseball with a passionate enthusiasm.

We played some evenings and on Sunday afternoons and we travelled considerable distances. I found that I could hit the ball naturally and easily but it was the fielding that I loved most of all. I played third base and the shortstop and I divided up our territory and responsibilities.

I would wait then for the bouncers and the line drives and the ground balls with delicious intensity. I would hope that each ball would be hit to me, and I do not recall any of them getting by. I would lunge and leap and bend and fall and pivot and turn and then hope that the next one might once again be mine. In my small area of the earth it seemed that everything was under my control.

The Tuning of Perfection

HE THOUGHT of himself, in the middle of that April, as a man who had made it through another winter. He was seventy-eight years old and it seems best to give his exact age now, rather than trying to rely on such descriptions as "old" or "vigorous" or "younger than his years." He was seventy-eight and a tall, slim man with dark hair and brown eyes and his own teeth. He was frequently described as "neat" because he always appeared clean-shaven and the clothes he wore were clean and in order. He wore suspenders instead of a belt because he felt they kept his trousers "in line" instead of allowing them to sag sloppily down his waist, revealing too much of his shirt. And when he went out in public, he always wore shoes. In cold or muddy weather, he wore overshoes or rubbers or what he called "overboots" – the rubber kind with the zippers in the front, to protect his shoes. He never wore the more common rubber boots in public – although, of course, he owned them and kept them neatly on a piece of clean cardboard in a corner of his porch.

He lived alone near the top of the mountain in a house which he himself had built when he was a much younger man. There had once been another house in the same clearing, and the hollow of its cellar was still visible as well as a few of the moss-covered stones which had formed its early foundation. This "ex-house" had been built by his great-grandfather shortly after he had come from the Isle of Skye and it was still referred to as "the first house" or sometimes as "the old house," although it was no longer there. No one was really sure why his great-grandfather had built the house so high up on the mountain, especially when one considered that he had been granted a great deal of land and there were more accessible spots upon it where one might build a house. Some thought that since he was a lumberman he had wanted to start on top of the mountain and log his way down. Others thought that because of the violence he had left in Scotland he wanted to be inaccessible in the new world and wanted to be able to see any potential enemies before they could see him. Others thought that he had merely wanted to be alone, while another group maintained that he had built it for the view. All of the reasons became confused and intermingled with the passing of the generations and the distancing of the man from Skye. Perhaps the theory of the view proved the most enduring because although the man from Skye and the house he built were no longer visible, the view still was. And it was truly spectacular. One could see for miles along the floor of the valley and over the tops of the smaller mountains and when one looked to the west there was the sea. There it was possible to see the various fishing boats of summer and the sealing ships of winter and the lines of Prince Edward Island and the flat shapes of the Magdalen Islands and, more to the east, the purple mass of Newfoundland.

The paved road or the "main road" which ran along the valley floor was five miles by automobile from his house, although it was not really that far if one walked and took various short cuts: paths and footbridges over the various tumbling brooks and creeks that spilled down the mountain's side. Once there had been a great deal of traffic on such paths, people on foot and people with horses, but over the years as more and more people obtained automobiles, the paths fell into disuse and became overgrown, and the bridges which were washed away by the spring freshets were no longer replaced very regularly or very well.

The section of winding road that led to his house and ended in his yard had been a bone of contention for many years, as had some of the other sections as well. Most of the people on the upper reaches of the mountain were his relatives and they were all on sections of the land granted to the man from Skye. Some of the road was "public" and therefore eligible to be maintained by the Department of Highways. Other sections of it, including his, were "private" so they were not maintained at all by government but only by the people living along them. As he lived a mile above the "second last" or the "second" house – depending upon which way you were counting – he did not receive visits from the grader or the gravel truck, or the snow plough in winter. It was generally assumed that the Department of Highways was secretly glad that it did not have to send its men or equipment up the twisting switchbacks and around the hairpin turns which skirted the treacherous gullies containing the wrecks of rolled and abandoned cars. The Department of Highways was not that fussy about the slightly lower reaches of the road either and there were always various petitions being circulated, demanding "better service for the tax dollar." Still, whenever the issue of making a "private" section of the road "public" was raised, there were always counter-petitions that circulated and used phrases like "keeping the land of our fathers *ours*." Three miles down the mountain, though (or two miles up), there was a nice wide "turn-around" for the school bus, and up to and including that spot the road was maintained as well as any other of its kind.

He did not mind living alone up on the mountain, saying that he got great television reception, which was of course true – although it was a relatively new justification. There was no television when he built the house in the two years prior to 1927 and when he was filled with the fever of his approaching marriage. Even then, people wondered why he was "going up the mountain" while many of the others were coming down, but he paid them little mind, working at it in determined perfection in the company of his twin brother and getting the others only when it was absolutely necessary: for the raising of the roof beams and the fitting of the gables.

He and his wife had been the same age and were almost consumed by one another while they were still quite young. Neither had ever had another boyfriend or girlfriend but he had told her they would not marry until he had completed the house. He wanted the house so that they could be "alone together" as soon as they were married, rather than moving in with in-laws or relatives for a while, as was frequently the custom of the time. So he had worked at it determinedly and desperately, anticipating the time when he could end "his life" and begin "their lives."

He and his twin brother had built it in "the old way," which meant making their own plans and cutting all the logs themselves and "snigging" them out with their horses and setting up their own saw mill and planing mill. And deciding also to use wooden pegs in the roof timbers instead of nails; so that the house would move in the mountain's winds – like a ship – move but not capsize, move yet still return.

In the summer before the marriage, his wife-to-be had worked as hard as he, carrying lumber and swinging a hammer; and when her father suggested she was doing too much masculine work, she had replied, "I am doing what I want to do. I am doing it for *us.*"

During the building of their house, they often sang together and the language of their singing was Gaelic. Sometimes one of them would sing the verses and the other the chorus and, at other times, they would sing the verses and choruses together and all the way through. Some of the songs contained at least fifteen or twenty verses and it would take a long time to complete them. On clear still days all of the people living down along the mountain's side and even below in the valley could hear the banging of their hammers and the youthful power of their voices.

They were married on a Saturday in late September and their first daughter was born exactly nine months later, which was an item of brief and passing interest. And their second daughter was born barely eleven months after their first. During the winter months of that time he worked in a lumber camp some fifteen miles away, cutting pulp for $1.75 a cord and getting $40.00 a month for his team of horses as well. Rising at five-thirty and working until after seven in the evening and sleeping on a bunk with a mattress made from boughs.

Sometimes he would come home on the weekends and on the clear, winter nights she would hear the distinctive sound of his horses' bells as they left the valley floor to begin their ascent up the mountain's side. Although the climb was steep, the horses would walk faster because they knew they were coming home, even breaking into a trot on the more level areas and causing their bells to accelerate accordingly. Sometimes he would get out of the wood sleigh and run beside the horses or ahead of them in order to keep warm and also to convince himself that he was getting home faster.

When she heard the bells she would take the lamp and move it from one window to the other and then take it back again and continue to repeat the procedure. The effect was almost that of a regularly flashing light, like that of a lighthouse or someone flicking a light switch off and on at regulated intervals. He would see the light now at one window and then in the other, sent down like the regulated flashing signals his mares gave off when in heat; and although he was exhausted, he would be filled with desire and urge himself upwards at an even greater rate.

After he had stabled his horses and fed them, he would go into their house and they would meet one another in the middle of the kitchen floor, holding and going into one another sometimes while the snow and frost still hung so heavily on his clothes that they creaked when he moved or steamed near the presence of the stove. The lamp would be stilled on the kitchen table and they would be alone. Only the monogamous eagles who nested in the hemlock tree even farther up the mountain seemed above them.

They were married for five years in an intensity which it seemed could never last, going more and more into each other and excluding most others for the company of themselves.

When she went into premature labour in February of 1931, he was not at home because it was still six weeks before the expected birth and they had decided that he would stay in the camp a little longer in order to earn the extra money they needed for their fourth child.

There had been heavy snows in the area and high winds and then it had turned bitterly cold, all in the span of a day and a half. It had been impossible to get down from the mountain and get word to him in the camp, although his twin brother managed to walk in on the second day, bringing him the news that everyone on the mountain already knew: that he had lost his wife and what might have been his first-born son. The snow was higher than his twin brother's head when they saw him coming into the camp. He was soaked with perspiration from fighting the drifts and pale and shaking and he began to throw up in the yard of the camp almost before he could deliver his message.

He had left immediately, leaving his brother behind to rest, while following his incoming tracks back out. He could not believe it, could not believe that she had somehow gone without him, could not believe that in their closeness he was still the last to know and that in spite of hoping "to live alone together" she had somehow died surrounded by others, but without him and really alone in the ultimate sense. He could not believe that in the closeness of their beginning there had been separation in their end. He had tried to hope that there might be some mistake; but the image of his brother, pale and shaken and vomiting in the packed-down snow of the lumber camp's yard, dispelled any such possibility.

He was numb throughout all of the funeral preparations and the funeral itself. His wife's sisters looked after his three small daughters who, while they sometimes called for their mother, seemed almost to welcome the lavish attention visited upon them. On the afternoon following the funeral the pneumonia which his twin brother had developed after his walk into the camp worsened and he had gone to sit beside his bed, holding his hand, at least able to be *present* this time, yet aware of the disapproving looks of Cora, his brother's wife, who was a woman he had never liked. Looks which said: If he had not gone for *you*, this would never have happened. Sitting there while his brother's chest deepened in spite of the poultices and the liniments and even the administrations of the doctor who finally made it up the mountain road and pronounced the pneumonia "surprisingly advanced."

After the death of his brother the numbness continued. He felt as those who lose all of their family in the midnight fire or on the sinking ship. Suddenly and without survivors. He felt guilt for his wife and for his brother's fatherless children and for his daughters who would now never know their mother. And he felt terribly alone.

His daughters stayed with him for a while as he tried to do what their mother had done. But gradually his wife's sisters began to suggest that the girls would be better off with them. At first he opposed the idea because both he and his wife had never been overly fond of her sisters, considering them somehow more vulgar than they were themselves. But gradually it became apparent that if he were ever to return to the woods and earn a living, someone would have to look after three children under the age of four. He was torn for the remainder of the winter months and into the spring, sometimes appreciating what he felt was the intended kindness of his in-laws and at other times angry at certain overheard remarks: "It is not right for three little girls to be alone up on that mountain with that man, a *young* man." As if he were more interesting as a potential child molester than simply as a father. Gradually his daughters began to spend evenings and weekends with their aunts and then weeks and then in the manner of small children, they no longer cried when he left, or clung to his legs, or sat in the window to await his approach. And then they began to call him "Archibald," as did the other members of the households in which they lived. So that in the end he seemed neither husband nor brother nor even father but only "Archibald." He was twenty-seven years old.

He had always been called Archibald or sometimes in Gaelic "Gilleasbuig." Perhaps because of what was perceived as a kind of formality that hung about him, no one ever called him "Arch" or the more familiar and common "Archie." He did not look or act "like an Archie," as they said. And with the passing of the years, letters came that were addressed simply to "Archibald" and which bore a variety of addresses covering a radius of some forty milles. Many of the letters in the later years came from the folklorists who had "discovered" him in the 1960s and for whom he had made various tapes and recordings. And he had come to be regarded as "the last of the authentic old-time Gaelic singers." He was faithfully recorded in the archives at Sydney and Halifax and Ottawa and his picture had appeared in various scholarly and less scholarly journals; sometimes with the arms of the folklorists around him, sometimes holding one of his horses and sometimes standing beside his shining pickup truck which bore a bumper sticker which read "Suas Leis A' Ghaidlig." Sometimes the articles bore titles such as "Cape Breton Singer: The Last of His Kind" or "Holding Fast on Top of the Mountain" or "Mnemonic Devices in the Gaelic Line" – the latter generally being accompanied by a plethora of footnotes.

He did not really mind the folklorists, enunciating the

words over and over again for them, explaining that "bh" was pronounced as "v" (like the "ph" in phone is pronounced "f," he would say), expanding on the more archaic meanings and footnoting himself the words and phrases of local origin. Doing it all with care and seriousness in much the same way that he filed and set his saws or structured his woodpile.

Now in this April of the 1980s he thought of himself, as I said earlier, as a man of seventy-eight years who had made it through another winter. He had come to terms with most things, although never really with the death of his wife; but that too had become easier during the last decades, although he was still bothered by the sexual references which came because of his monastic existence.

Scarcely a year after "the week of deaths," he had been visited by Cora, his twin brother's wife. She had come with her breath reeking of rum and placed the bottle on the middle of his kitchen table.

"I've been thinking," she said. "It's time me and you got together."

"Mmmm," he said, trying to make the most non-committal sound he could think of.

"Here," she said, going to his cupboard and taking down two of his sparkling glasses and splashing rum into them. "Here," she said, sliding a glass towards him across the table and seating herself opposite him. "Here, have a shot of this. It will put lead in your pencil," and then after a pause, "although from what I've *heard* there's no need of that."

He was taken aback, somehow imagining her and his twin brother lying side by side at night discussing his physicality.

Heard *what?* he wondered. *Where?*

"Yeah," she said. "There's not much need of you being up here on this mountain by yourself and me being by myself farther down. If you don't use it, it'll rust off."

He was close to panic, finding her so lonely and so drunkenly available and so much unlike the memory of his own wife. He wondered if she remembered how much they disliked each other, or thought they did. And he wondered if he were somehow thought of as being interchangeable with his dead brother. As if, because they were twins, their bodies must somehow be the same, regardless of their minds.

"I bet it's rusty right now," she said and she leaned the upper part of her body across the table so that he could smell the rum heavy on her breath even as he felt her fingers on his leg.

"Mmmm," he said, getting up rapidly and walking towards the window. He was rattled by her overt sexuality, the way a shy middle-aged married man might be when taken on a visit to a brothel far from his home – not because what is discussed is so foreign to him, but rather because of the manner and the approach.

Outside the window the eagles were flying up the mountain, carrying the twigs, some of them almost branches, for the building of their home.

"Mmmm," he said, looking out the window and down the winding road to the valley floor below.

"Well," she said, getting up and downing her drink. "I guess there's no fun here. I just wanted to say hello."

"Yes," he said. "Well, thank you."

She lurched towards the door and he wondered if he should open it for her or if that would be too rash.

But she opened it herself.

"Well," she said as she went out into the yard. "You know where I'm at."

"Yes," he said, gaining confidence from her departing back, "I know where you are."

Now on this morning in April half a century later, he looked out his window at the eagles flying by. They were going down into the valley to hunt, leaving their nest with their four precious eggs for the briefest time. Then he recognized the sound of a truck's motor. He recognized it before it entered the yard, in the way his wife had once recognized the individual sound of his horses' bells. The truck was muddy and splattered, not merely from this spring trip up the mountain but from a sort of residual dirt perhaps from the previous fall. It belonged to his married granddaughter who had been christened Sarah but preferred to be known as Sal. She wheeled her truck into the yard, getting out of it inches from his door and almost before it had stopped. She wore her hair in a ponytail, although she seemed too old for that, and her tight-fitting jeans were slipped inside her husband's rubber boots. He was always slightly surprised at her ability to chew gum and smoke cigarettes at the same time and was reminded of that now as she came through his door, her lipstick leaving a red ring around her cigarette as she removed it from her mouth and flicked it out into the yard. She wore a tight-fitting T-shirt with the words "I'm Busted" across her chest.

"Hi, Archibald," she said, sitting in the chair nearest the window.

"Hi," he said.

"What's new?"

"Oh, nothing much," he replied, and then after a pause, "Would you like some tea?"

"Okay," she said. "No milk. I'm watching my figure."

"Mmmm," he said.

He looked at her from the distance of his years, trying to find within her some flashes of his wife or even of himself. She was attractive in her way, with her dark eyes and ready mouth, although shorter than either he or his wife.

"Had two phone calls," she said.

"Oh," he said, always feeling a bit guilty that he had no telephone and that messages had to be left with others farther down the mountain.

"One is from a guy who wants to buy your mare. You're still interested in selling?"

"Yes, I guess so."

"The other is about Gaelic singing. They want us to sing in Halifax this summer. This is the year of 'Scots Around the World.' All kinds of people will be there, even some of the Royal Family. We'll be there for a week. They haven't decided on the pay yet but it'll be okay and they'll pay our accommodation and our transportation."

"Oh," he said, becoming interested and cautious at the same time. "What do you mean by us?"

"*Us.* You know, the family. They want twenty of us. There'll be a few days of rehearsal there and then some concerts and we'll be on television. I can hardly wait. I have to do lots of shopping in Halifax and it will be a chance to sleep in without Tom bothering me. We won't even have to be at the theatre or studio or whatever until noon." She lit another cigarette.

"What do they want us to sing?" he asked.

"Oh, who cares?" she said. "It's the trip that's important. Some of the old songs. They're coming to audition us or something in two or three weeks. We'll sing *Fear A' Bhata* or something," she said, and butting her cigarette on her saucer and laying her gum beside it on the table, she began to sing in a clear, powerful voice:

> *Fhir a' bhata, na ho ro eile,*
> *Fhir a' bhata, na ho ro eile,*
> *Fhir a' bhata, na ho ro eile,*
> *Mho shoraidh slan leat 's gach ait' an teid thu*
>
> *Is tric mi 'sealltainn o 'n chnoc a 's airde*
> *Dh'fheuch am faic mi fear a' bhata,*
> *An tig thu 'n diugh, no 'n tig thu 'maireach;*
> *'S mur tig thu idir, gur truagh a tha mi.*

Only when she sang did she remind him somewhat of his wife, and again he felt the hope that she might reach that standard of excellence.

"You're singing it too fast," he said cautiously when she had finished. "But it is good. You're singing it like a milling song. It's supposed to be a lament for a loved one that's lost."

He sang it himself slowly, stressing the distinction of each syllable.

She seemed interested for a while, listening intently before replacing her gum and lighting another cigarette, then tossing the still-lighted match into the stove.

"Do you know what the words mean?" he said when he had finished.

"No," she said. "Neither will anybody else. I just make the noises. I've been hearing the things since I was two. I know how they go. I'm not dumb, you know."

"Who else are they asking?" he said, partially out of interest and partially to change the subject and avoid confrontation.

"I don't know. They said they'd get back to us later. All they wanted to know now was if we were interested. The man about the mare will be up later. I got to go now."

She was out of the door almost immediately, turning her truck in a spray of gravel that flicked against his house, the small stones pinging against his windowpane. A muddied bumper sticker read: "If you're horny, honk your horn."

He was reminded, as he often was, of Cora, who had been dead now for some fifteen years and who had married another man within a year of her visit to him with her open proposal. And he was touched that his granddaughter should seem so much like his brother's wife instead of like his own.

The man who came to buy the mare was totally unlike any other horse buyer he had ever seen. He came in a suit and in an elaborate car and spoke in an accent that was difficult to identify. He was accompanied by Carver, who was apparently his guide, a violent young man in his thirties from the other side of the mountain. Carver's not-unhandsome face was marred by a series of raised grey scars and his upper lip had been thickened as a result of a fight in which someone had swung a logging chain into his mouth, an action which had also cost him his most obvious teeth. He wore his wallet on a chain hooked to his belt and scuffed his heavy lumberman's boots on the cardboard in Archibald's porch before entering the kitchen. He was by the window and rolled a cigarette while the horse buyer talked to Archibald.

"How old is the mare?"

"Five," said Archibald.

"Has she ever had a colt?"

"Why, yes," said Archibald, puzzled by the question. Usually buyers asked if the horse would work single or double or something about its disposition or its legs or chest. Or if it would work in snow or eat enough to sustain a heavy work schedule.

"Do you think she could have another colt?" he asked.

"Why, I suppose," he said, almost annoyed, "if she had a stallion."

"No problem," said the man.

"But," said Archibald, driven by his old honesty, "she has never worked. I have not been in the woods that much lately and I always used the old mare, her mother, before she died. I planned to train her but never got around to it. She's more like a pet. She probably will work, though. They've always worked. It's in the stock. I've had them all my life." He stopped, almost embarrassed at having to apologize for his horses and for himself.

"Okay," said the man. "No problem. She has had a colt, though?"

"Look," said Carver from his seat near the window, snuffing out his cigarette between his callused thumb and forefinger, "he already told you that. I told you this man don't lie."

"Okay," said the man, taking out his chequebook.

"Don't you want to see her first?" asked Archibald.

"No, it's okay," the man said. "I believe you."

"He wants nine hundred dollars," said Carver. "She's a young mare."

"Okay," said the man, to Archibald's amazement. He had been hopeful of perhaps seven hundred dollars or even less since she had never worked.

"You'll take her down in your truck later?" the man said to Carver.

"Right on!" said Carver and they left, the man driving with a peculiar caution as if he had never been off pavement before and was afraid that the woods might swallow him.

After they left, Archibald went out to his barn to talk to the mare. He led her out to the brook to drink, then to the door of the house where she waited while he went in and rummaged for some bread to offer her as a farewell treat. She was young and strong and splendid and he was somehow disappointed that the buyer had not at least seen her so that he could appreciate her excellent qualities.

Shortly after noon Carver drove his truck into the yard. "Do you want a beer?" he said to Archibald, motioning towards the open case on the seat beside him.

"No, I don't think so," Archibald said. "We may as well get this over with."

"Okay," said Carver. "Do you want to lead her on?"

"No, it's okay," said Archibald. "She'll go with anybody."

"Yeah," said Carver. "Perhaps that's a good way to be."

They went into the barn. In spite of what he had said, Archibald found himself going up beside the mare and untying the rope and leading her out into the afternoon sun which reflected on her dappled shining coat. Carver backed his truck up to a small incline beside the barn and lowered the tailgate. Then Archibald handed him the rope and watched as she followed him willingly into the truck.

"This is the last of all them nice horses you had up here,

eh?" said Carver after he had tied the rope and swung down from the truck.

"Yes," said Archibald, "the last."

"I guess you hauled a lot of wood with them horses. I heard guys talking, older guys who worked with you in the camps."

"Oh, yes," said Archibald.

"I heard guys say you and your brother could cut seven cords of pulp a day with a crosscut saw, haul it and stack it."

"Oh, yes," he said. "Some days we could. Days seemed longer then," he added with a smile.

"Christ, we're lucky to get seven with a power saw unless we're in a real good stand," said Carver, pulling up his trousers and starting to roll a cigarette. "Your timber here on your own land is as good as ever, they say."

"Yes," he said. "It's pretty good."

" 'That Archibald,' they say, 'no one knows where he gets all them logs, hauls them out with them horses and doesn't seem to disturb anything. Year after year. Treats the mountain as if it were a garden.' "

"Mmmm," he said.

"Not like now, eh? We just cut 'em all down. Go in with heavy equipment, tree farmers and loaders and do it all in a day, to hell with tomorrow."

"Yes," said Archibald. "I've noticed."

"You don't want to sell?" asked Carver.

"No," he said. "Not yet."

"I just thought … since you were letting your mare go. No work for the mare, no work for you."

"Oh, she'll probably work somewhere," he said. "I'm not so sure about myself."

"Nah, she won't work," said Carver. "They want her for birth control pills."

"For what?" said Archibald.

"This guy says, I don't know if it's true, that there's this farm outside of Montreal that's connected to a lab or something.

Anyway, they've got all these mares there and they keep them bred all the time and they use their water for birth control pills."

It seemed so preposterous that Archibald was not sure how to react. He scrutinized Carver's scarred yet open face, looking for a hint, some kind of touch, but he could find nothing.

"Yeah," said Carver. "They keep the mares pregnant all the time so the women won't be."

"What do they do with the colts?" said Archibald, thinking that he might try a question for a change.

"I dunno," said Carver. "He didn't say. I guess they just throw them away. Got to go now," he said, swinging into the cab of his truck, "and take her down the mountain. I think he's almost got a boxcar of these mares, or a transport truck. In two days she'll be outside Montreal and they'll get her a stallion and that'll be it."

The truck roared into action and moved from the incline near the barn. Archibald had been closer to it than he thought and was forced to step out of the way. As it passed, Carver rolled down the window and shouted, "Hey, Archibald, do you sing anymore?"

"Not so much," he said.

"Got to talk to you about that sometime," he said above the engine's roar and then he and the truck and the splendid mare left the yard to begin their switchbacked journey down the mountain.

For a long time Archibald did not know what to do. He felt somehow betrayed by forces he could not control. The image of his mare beneath the weight of successive and different stallions came to his mind but the most haunting image was that of the dead colts which Carver had described as being "thrown away." He imagined them as the many dead unwanted animals he had seen thrown out on the manure piles behind the barns, their skulls smashed in by blows from axes. He doubted that there was anything like that outside of Montreal and he doubted – or wanted to doubt – somehow more than he could what Carver had said. But he had no way to verify the facts or disprove them, and the images persisted. He thought, as he always did at times of loss, of his wife. And then of the pale, still body of his quiet and unbreathing son, with the intricate blue veins winding like the map lines of roads and rivers upon his fragile, delicate skull. Both wife and son gone from him, taken in the winter's snow. And he felt somehow that he might cry.

He looked up to the sound of the whooshing eagles' wings. They were flying up the mountain, almost wavering in their flight. Like weary commuters trying to make it home. He had watched them through the long winter as they were forced to fly farther and farther in search of food and open water. He had noticed the dullness of their feathers and the dimming lustre in their intense green eyes. Now, and he was not sure if perhaps it was his eyesight or his angle of vision, the female's wing tips seemed almost to graze the bare branches of the trees as if she might falter and fall. And then the male who had gone on ahead turned and came back, gliding on the wind with his wings outstretched, trying to conserve what little energy he had left. He passed so close to Archibald that he could see, or imagined that he could see, the desperate fear in his fierce, defiant eyes. He was so intent on his mission that he paid little attention to Archibald, circling beside his mate until their wing tips almost touched. She seemed to gain strength from his presence and almost to lunge with her wings, like a desperate swimmer on her final lap, and they continued together up the mountain. In the dampness of the late spring Archibald feared, as perhaps did they, for the future of their potential young.

He had seen the eagles in other seasons and circumstances. He had seen the male seize a branch in his powerful talons and soar towards the sky in the sheer exuberance of his power and strength; had seen him snap the branch in two (in the way a strong man might snap a kindling across his knee), letting the two sections fall towards the earth before plummeting after one or the other and snatching it from the air; wheeling and somersaulting and flipping the branch in front of him and swooping under it again and again until, tired of the game, he let it fall to earth.

And he had seen them in the aerial courtship of their mating; had seen them feinting and swerving high above the mountain, outlined against the sky. Had seen them come together, and with talons locked, fall cartwheeling over and over for what seemed like hundreds of feet down towards the land. Separating and braking, like lucky parachutists, at the last minute and gliding individually and parallel to the earth before starting their ascent once more.

The folklorists were always impressed by the bald eagles.

"How long have they been here?" the first group asked.

"Forever, I guess," had been his answer.

And after doing research they had returned and said, "Yes, Cape Breton is the largest nesting area on the eastern seaboard north of Florida. And the largest east of the Rockies. It's funny, hardly anybody knows they're here."

"Oh, some people do," Archibald said with a smile.

"It's only because they don't use pesticides or herbicides in the forest industry," the folklorists said. "If they start, the eagles will be gone. There are hardly any nests anymore in New Brunswick or in Maine."

"Mmmm," he said.

In the days that followed they tried to prepare for the "singing" in Halifax. They had several practices, most of them at Sal's because she had talked to the producer and had become the contact person and also because she seemed to want to go the most. They managed to gather a number of people of varying talent, some more reluctant than others. One or two of the practices were held at Archibald's. The number in the group varied. It expanded sometimes to as many as thirty, including various in-laws and friends of in-laws and people who simply had little else to do on a given evening. Throughout it all, Archibald tried to maintain control and to do it in "his way," which meant enunciating the words clearly and singing the exact number of verses in the proper order. Sometimes the attention of the younger people wandered and the evenings deteriorated quite early and rapidly, with people drifting off into little knots to gossip or tell jokes or to drink what was in Archibald's opinion too much. As the pressures of the spring season increased and many of the men left logging to fish or work upon their land, there were fewer and fewer male voices at the practice sessions. Sometimes the men joked about this and the future make-up of the group.

"Do you think you'll be able to handle all these women by yourself in Halifax, Archibald?" someone might ask, although not really asking the question of him.

"Sure, he will," another voice would respond. "He's well rested. He hasn't used it in fifty years – not that we know of, anyway."

Then at one practice Sal announced with some agitation that she had been talking to the producer in Halifax. He had told her, she said, that two other groups from the area had contacted him and he would be auditioning them as well. He would be coming in about ten days.

Everyone was dumbfounded.

"What other groups?" asked Archibald.

"One," said Sal, pausing for dramatic effect, "is headed by *Carver*."

"Carver!" they said in unison and disbelief. And then in the midst of loud guffaws, "Carver can't sing. He can hardly speak any Gaelic. Where will he get a group?"

"Don't ask me," said Sal, "unless it's those guys he hangs around with."

"Who else?" said Archibald.

"MacKenzies!" she said.

No one laughed at the mention of MacKenzies. They had been one of the oldest and best of the singing families. They lived some twenty miles away in a small and isolated valley, but Archibald had noticed, over the past fifteen years or so, more and more of their houses becoming shuttered and boarded and a few of the older ones starting to lean and even to fall to the pressures of the wind.

"They don't have enough people anymore," someone said.

"No," added another voice. "All of their best singers have gone to Toronto."

"There are two very good young men there," said Archibald, remembering a concert of a few years back when he had seen the two standing straight and tall a few feet back from the microphone, had seen them singing clearly and effortlessly with never a waver or a mispronunciation or a missed note.

"They've gone to Calgary," said a third voice. "They've been there now for over a year."

"I was talking to some people from over that way after the call from Halifax," said Sal. "They said that the MacKenzies' grandmother was going to ask them to come back. They said she was going to try to get all her singers to come home."

Archibald was touched in spite of himself, touched that Mrs. MacKenzie would try so hard. He looked around the room and realized that there were very few people in it who knew that Mrs. MacKenzie was his cousin and by extension theirs. Although he did not know her well and had only nodded to her and exchanged a few words with her over a lifetime, he felt very close to her now. He was not even sure of the degree of the relationship (although he would work it out later), remembering only the story of the young woman from an earlier generation of his family who had married the young man from the valley of the MacKenzies who was of the "wrong religion." There had been great bitterness at the time and the families had refused to speak to one another until all those who knew what the "right religion" was had died. The young woman who left had never visited her parents or they her. It seemed sad to Archibald, feeling almost more kinship to the scarcely known Mrs. MacKenzie than to those members of his own flesh and blood who seemed now so agitated and squabbly.

"She will never get them home," said the last voice. "They've all got jobs and responsibilities. They can't drop everything and come here or to Halifax for a week to sing four or five songs."

The voice proved right, although in the following ten days before the producer's visit Archibald thought often of Mrs. MacKenzie making her phone calls and of her messengers fanned out across Toronto, visiting the suburbs and the taverns, asking the question to which they already knew the answer but feeling obliged to ask it, nonetheless. In the end four MacKenzies came home, two young men who had been hurt at work and were on compensation and a middle-aged daughter and her husband who managed to take a week of their vacation earlier than usual. The *really* good young men were unable to come.

When the producer came he brought with him two male assistants with clipboards. The producer was an agitated man in his early thirties. He had dark curly hair and wore thick glasses and a maroon T-shirt with "If you've got it, flaunt it" emblazoned across the front. When he spoke, he nervously twisted his right ear lobe.

Archibald's group was the last of the three he visited. "He's saved the best for the last," laughed Sal, not very convincingly.

He came in the evening and explained the situation briefly. If chosen, they would be in Halifax for six days. They would practise and acquaint themselves with the surroundings for the first two days and on the next four there would be a concert each evening. There would be various acts from throughout the province. They would be on television and radio and some of the Royal Family would be in attendance.

Then he said, "Look, I really don't understand your language so we're here mainly to look for effect. We'd like you to be ready with three songs. And then maybe we'll have to cut it back to two. We'll see how it goes."

They began to sing, sitting around the table as if they were "waulking the cloth," as their ancestors had done before them. Archibald sat at the head of the table, singing loudly and clearly, while the other voices rose to meet him. The producer and his assistants took notes.

"Okay, that's enough," he said after about an hour and a half.

"We'll take the third one," he said to one of his assistants.

"What's it called?" he asked Archibald.

"*Mo Chridhe Trom*," said Archibald. "It means my heart is heavy."

"Okay," said the producer. "Let's do it again."

They began. By the twelfth verse the music took hold of Archibald in a way that he had almost forgotten it could. His voice soared above the others with such clear and precise power that they faltered and were stilled.

> *'S ann air cul nam beanntan ard,*
> *Tha aite comhnuidh mo ghraidh,*
> *Fear dha 'm bheil an chridhe blath,*
> *Do 'n tug mi 'n gradh a leon mi.*
>
> *'S ann air cul a' bhalla chloich,*
> *'S math an aithnichinn lorg do chos,*
> *Och 'us och, mar tha mi 'n nochd*
> *Gur bochd nach d'fhuair mi coir ort.*
>
> *Tha mo chridhe dhut cho buan,*
> *Ris a' chreag tha 'n grunnd a' chuain,*
> *No comh-ionnan ris an stuaidh*
> *A bhuaileas orr' an comhnuidh.*

He finished the song alone. There was a silence that was almost embarrassing.

"Okay," said the producer after a pause. "Try another one, number six. The one that doesn't sound like all the others. What's it called?"

"*Oran Gillean Alasdair Mhoir*," said Archibald, trying to compose himself. "Song to the Sons of Big Alexander. Sometimes it's known simply as The Drowning of the Men."

"Okay," said the producer. "Let's go." But when they were halfway through, he said, "Cut, okay, that's enough."

"It's not finished," said Archibald. "It's a narrative."

"That's enough," said the producer.

"You can't cut them like that," said Archibald, "if you do, they don't make any sense."

"Look, they don't make any sense to me, anyway," said the producer. "I told you I don't understand the language. We're just trying to gauge audience impact."

Archibald felt himself getting angrier than perhaps he should, and he was aware of the looks and gestures from his family. "Be careful," they said, "don't offend him or we won't get the trip."

"Mmmm," he said, rising from his chair and going to the window. The dusk had turned to dark and the stars seemed to touch the mountain. Although in a room filled with people, he felt very much alone, his mind running silently over the verses of *Mo Chridhe Trom* which had so moved him moments before.

> *Over lofty mountains lies*
> *The dwelling place of my love,*
> *One whose heart was always warm,*
> *And whom I loved too dearly.*
>
> *And behind the wall of stone*
> *I would recognize your steps,*

But how sad am I tonight
Because we're not together.

Still my love you will last
Like the rock beneath the sea,
Just as long as will the waves
That strike against it always.

"Okay, let's call it a night," said the producer. "Thank you all very much. We'll be in touch."

The next morning at nine the producer drove into Archibald's yard. His assistants were with him, packed and ready for Halifax. The assistants remained in the car while the producer came into Archibald's kitchen. He coughed uncomfortably and looked about him as if to make sure that they were alone. He reminded Archibald of a nervous father preparing to discuss "the facts of life."

"How were the other groups?" asked Archibald in what he hoped was a noncommittal voice.

"The young man Carver and his group," said the producer, "have tremendous *energy*. They have a lot of male voices."

"Mmmm," said Archibald. "What did they sing?"

"I don't remember the names of the songs, although I wrote them down. They're packed away. It doesn't matter all that much, anyway. They don't know as many songs as you people do, though," he concluded.

"No," said Archibald, trying to restrain his sarcasm, "I don't suppose they do."

"Still, that doesn't matter so much either as we only need two or three."

"Mmmm."

"The problem with that group is the way they look."

"The way they *look*?" said Archibald. "Shouldn't it be the way they sing?"

"Not really," said the producer. "See, these performances

have a high degree of *visibility*. You're going to be on stage for four nights and the various television networks are all going to be there. This is, in total, a *big show*. It's not a regional show. It will be national and international. It will probably be beamed back to Scotland and Australia and who knows where else. We want people who *look right* and who'll give a good impression of the area and the province."

Archibald said nothing.

"You see," said the producer, "we've got to have someone we can zoom in on for close-ups, someone who looks the part. We don't want close-ups of people who have had their faces all carved up in brawls. That's why you're so good. You're a great-looking man for your age, if you'll pardon me. You're tall and straight and have your own teeth, which helps both your singing and appearance. You have a *presence*. The rest of your group have nice voices, especially the women, but without you, if you'll pardon me, they're kind of ordinary. And then," he added almost as an afterthought, "there is your reputation. You're known to the folklorists and people like that. You have *credibility*. Very important."

Archibald was aware of Sal's truck coming into the yard and knew that she had seen the producer's car on its way up the mountain.

"Hi," she said, "what's new?"

"I think you're all set but it's up to your grandfather," the producer said.

"What about the MacKenzies?" asked Archibald.

"Garbage. No good at all. An old woman playing a tape recorder while seven or eight people tried to sing along with it. Wasted our time. We wanted people that were *alive*, not some scratchy tape."

"Mmmm," said Archibald.

"Anyway, you're on. But we'd like a few changes."

"Changes?"

"Yeah, first of all we'll have to cut them. That was what I was trying to get around to last night. You're only going to be on stage for three or four minutes each night and we'd like to get two songs in. They're too long. The other problem is they're too mournful. Jesus, even the titles, 'My Heart is Heavy,' 'The Drowning of the Men.' Think about it."

"But," said Archibald, trying to sound reasonable, "that's the way those songs are. You've got to hear them in the original way."

"I've got to go now," said Sal. "Got to see about babysitters and that. See you."

She left in her customary spray of gravel.

"Look," said the producer, "I've got to put on a big show. Maybe you could get some songs from the other group."

"The other group?"

"Yeah," he said, "Carver's. Anyway, think about it. I'll call you in a week and we can finalize it and work out any other details." And then he was gone.

In the days that followed Archibald *did* think about it. He thought about it more than he had ever thought he would. He thought of the impossibility of trimming the songs and of changing them and he wondered why he seemed the only one in his group who harboured such concerns. Most of the others did not seem very interested when he mentioned it to them, although they did seem interested in shopping lists and gathering the phone numbers of long-absent relatives and friends in Halifax.

One evening Carver met Sal on her way to Bingo and told her quite bluntly that he and his group were going.

"No, you're not," she said, "we are."

"Wait and see," said Carver. "Look, we need this trip. We need to get a boat engine and we want to buy a truck. You guys are done. Done like a dinner. It matters too much to that Archibald and you're all dependent on him. *Us*, we're *adjustable*."

"As if we couldn't be adjustable!" said Sal with a laugh as

she told of the encounter at their last practice before the anticipated phone call. The practice did not go well as far as Archibald was concerned, although no one else seemed to notice.

The next day when Archibald encountered Carver at the general store down in the valley, he could not resist asking: "What did you sing for that producer fellow?"

"*Brochan Lom*," said Carver with a shrug.

"*Brochan Lom*," said Archibald incredulously. "Why, that isn't even a song. It's just a bunch of nonsense syllables strung together."

"So what!" said Carver. "He didn't know. No one knows."

"But it's before the Royal Family," said Archibald, surprising even himself at finding such royalist remnants still within him.

"Look," said Carver, wiping his mouth with the back of his hand, "what did the Royal Family ever do for *me*?"

"Of course people know," said Archibald, pressing on with weary determination. "People in audiences know. Other singers know. Folklorists know."

"Yeah, maybe so," said Carver with a shrug, "but me, I don't know no folklorists."

He looked at Archibald intently for a few seconds and then gathered up his tobacco and left the store.

Archibald was troubled all of that afternoon. He was vaguely aware of his relatives organizing sitters and borrowing suitcases and talking incessantly but saying little. He thought of his conversation with Carver, on the one hand, and strangely enough, he thought of Mrs. MacKenzie on the other. He thought of her with great compassion, she who was probably the best of them all and who had tried the hardest to impress the man from Halifax. The image of her in the twilight of the valley of the MacKenzies playing the tape-recorded voices of her departed family to a man who did not know the language kept running through his mind. He imagined her now, sitting quietly with her knitting needles in her lap, listening to the ghostly voices which were there without their people.

And then that night Archibald had a dream. He had often had dreams of his wife in the long, long years since her death and had probably brought them on in the early years by visiting her grave in the evenings and sometimes sitting there and talking to her of their hopes and aspirations. And sometimes in the nights following such "conversations" she would come to him and they would talk and touch and sometimes sing. But on this night she only sang. She sang with a clarity and a beauty that caused the hairs to rise on the back of his neck even as the tears welled to his eyes. Every note was perfect, as perfect and clear as the waiting water droplet hanging on the fragile leaf or the high suspended eagle outlined against the sky at the apex of its arc. She sang to him until four in the morning when the first rays of light began to touch the mountain top. And then she was gone.

Archibald awoke relaxed and refreshed in a way that he had seldom felt since sleeping with his wife so many years before. His mind was made up and he was done thinking about it.

Around nine o'clock Sal's truck came into the yard. "That producer fellow is on the phone," she said. "I told him I'd take the message but he wants to talk to you."

"Okay," said Archibald.

In Sal's kitchen the receiver swung from its black spiral cord.

"Yes, this is Archibald," he said, grasping it firmly. "No, I don't think I can get them down to three minutes or speed them up at all. No, I don't think so. Yes, I have thought about it. Yes, I have been in contact with others who sing in my family. No, I don't know about Carver. You'll have to speak to him. Thank you. Good-bye."

He was aware of the disappointment and grumpiness that

spread throughout the house, oozing like a rapid ink across a blotter. In the next room he heard a youthful voice say: "All he had to do was shorten the verses in a few stupid, old songs. You'd think he would have done it for *us*, the old coot."

"I'm sorry," he said to Sal, "but I just couldn't do it."

"Do you want a drive home in the truck?" she asked.

"No," he said, "never mind, I can walk."

He began to walk up the mountain with an energy and purpose that reminded him of himself as a younger man. He felt that he was "right" in the way he had felt so many years before when he had courted his future bride and when they had decided to build their house near the mountain's top even though others were coming down. And he felt as he had felt during the short and burning intensity of their brief life together. He began almost to run.

In the days that followed, Archibald was at peace. One day Sal dropped in and said that Carver was growing a moustache and a beard.

"They told him the moustache would cover his lip and with the beard his scars would be invisible on TV," she sniffed. "Make-up will do wonders."

Then one rainy night after he was finished watching the international and national and regional news, Archibald looked out his window. Down on the valley floor he could see the headlights of the cars following the wet pavement of the main highway. People bound for larger destinations who did not know that he existed. And then he noticed one set of lights in particular. They were coming hard and fast along the valley floor and although still miles away, they seemed to be coming with a purpose all their own. They "looked" different from the other headlights and in one of those moments of knowledge mixed with intuition Archibald said aloud to himself: "That car is coming here. It is coming for *me*."

He was rattled at first. He was aware that his decision had caused ill feelings among some members of his family as well as various in-laws and others strung out in a far-flung and complicated web of connections he could barely comprehend. He knew also that because of the rain many of the men had not been in the woods that much lately and were perhaps spending their time in the taverns talking too much about him and what he had done. He watched as the car swung off the pavement and began its ascent, weaving and sloughing up the mountain in the rain.

Although he was not a violent man, he did not harbour any illusions about where or how he lived. "That Archibald," they said, "is nobody's fool." He thought of this now as he measured the steps to the stove where the giant poker hung. He had had it made by a blacksmith in one of the lumber camps shortly after his marriage. It was of heavy steel, and years of poking it into the hot coals of his stove had sharpened its end to a clean and burnished point. When he swung it in his hand its weight seemed like an ancient sword. He lifted his wooden table easily and placed it at an angle which he hoped was not too obvious in the centre of the kitchen, with its length facing the door.

"If they come in the door," he said, "I will be behind the table and in five strides I can reach the poker." He practised the five strides just to make sure. Then he put his left hand between his legs to adjust himself and straightened his suspenders so that they were perfectly in line. And then he went to the side of the window to watch the coming car.

Because of the recent rains, sections of the road had washed away and at certain places freshets and small brooks cut across it. Sometimes the rains washed down sand and topsoil as well, and the trick was never to accelerate on such washed-over sections for fear of being buried in the flowing water and mud. Rather, one gunned the motor on the relatively stable sections of the climb (where there was "bottom") and trusted to momentum to get across the streams.

Archibald watched the progress of the car. Sometimes he

lost its headlights because of his perspective and the trees, but only momentarily. As it climbed, swerving back and forth, the wet branches slapping and silhouetted against its headlights, Archibald began to read the dark wet roadway in his own mind. And he began to read the driver's reflexes as he swung out from the gullies and then in close to the mountain's wall. He began almost to admire the driver. Whoever that is, he thought, is very drunk but also very good.

The car hooked and turned into his yard without any apparent change in speed, its headlights flashing on his house and through his window. Archibald moved behind his table and stood, tall and balanced and ready. Before the sound of the slamming car door faded, his kitchen door seemed to blow in and Carver stood there unsteadily, blinking in the light with the rain blowing at his back and dripping off his beginning beard.

"Yeah," he said over his shoulder, "he's here, bring it in."

Archibald waited, his eyes intent upon Carver but also sliding sideways to his poker.

They came into his porch and there were five of them, carrying boxes.

"Put them on the floor here," said Carver, indicating a space just across the threshold. "And try not to dirty his floor."

Archibald knew then he would be all right and moved out from behind his table.

"Open the boxes," said Carver to one of the men. The boxes were filled with forty-ounce bottles of liquor. It was as if someone were preparing for a wedding.

"These are for you," said Carver. "We bought them at a bootlegger's two hours ago. We been away all day. We been to Glace Bay and to New Waterford and we were in a fight in the parking lot at the tavern in Bras D'Or, and a couple of us got banged up pretty bad. Anyway, not much to say."

Archibald looked at them framed in the doorway leading to his porch. There was no mystery about the kind of day they had had, even if Carver had not told him. Even now, one of them, a tall young man, was rocking backwards on his heels, almost literally falling asleep on his feet as he stood in the doorway. There was a fresh cut on Carver's temple which could not be covered by either his moustache or his beard. Archibald looked at all the liquor and was moved by the total inappropriateness of the gift; bringing all of this to him, the most abstemious man on the mountain. Somehow it moved him even more. And he was aware of its cost in many ways.

He also envied them their closeness and their fierceness and what the producer fellow had called their tremendous energy. And he imagined it was men like they who had given, in their recklessness, all they could think of in that confused and stormy past. Going with their claymores and the misunderstood language of their war cries to "perform" for the Royal Families of the past. But he was not sure of that either. He smiled at them and gave a small nod of acknowledgement. He did not quite know what to say.

"Look," said Carver, with that certainty that marked everything he did. "Look, Archibald," he said. "We know. We know. We *really* know."

As Birds Bring Forth the Sun

ONCE THERE WAS a family with a Highland name who lived beside the sea. And the man had a dog of which he was very fond. She was large and grey, a sort of staghound from another time. And if she jumped up to lick his face, which she loved to do, her paws would jolt against his shoulders with such force that she would come close to knocking him down and he would be forced to take two or three backward steps before he could regain his balance. And he himself was not a small man, being slightly over six feet and perhaps one hundred and eighty pounds.

She had been left, when a pup, at the family's gate in a small handmade box and no one knew where she had come from or that she would eventually grow to such a size. Once, while still a small pup, she had been run over by the steel wheel of a horse-drawn cart which was hauling kelp from the shore to be used as fertilizer. It was in October and the rain had been falling for some weeks and the ground was soft. When the wheel of the cart passed over her, it sunk her body into the wet earth as well as crushing some of her ribs; and apparently the silhouette of her small crushed body was visible in the earth after the man lifted her to his chest while she yelped and screamed. He ran his fingers along her broken bones, ignoring the blood and urine which fell upon his shirt, trying to soothe her bulging eyes and her scrabbling front paws and her desperately licking tongue.

The more practical members of his family, who had seen run-over dogs before, suggested that her neck be broken by his strong hands or that he grasp her by the hind legs and swing her head against a rock, thus putting an end to her misery. But he would not do it.

Instead, he fashioned a small box and lined it with woollen remnants from a sheep's fleece and one of his old and frayed shirts. He placed her within the box and placed the box behind the stove and then he warmed some milk in a small saucepan and sweetened it with sugar. And he held open her small and trembling jaws with his left hand while spooning in the sweetened milk with his right, ignoring the needle-like sharpness of her small teeth. She lay in the box most of the remaining fall and into the early winter, watching everything with her large brown eyes.

Although some members of the family complained about her presence and the odour from the box and the waste of time she involved, they gradually adjusted to her; and as the weeks passed by, it became evident that her ribs were knitting together in some form or other and that she was recovering with the resilience of the young. It also became evident that she would grow to a tremendous size, as she outgrew one box and then another and the grey hair began to feather from her huge front paws. In the spring she was outside almost all of the time and followed the man everywhere; and when she came inside during the following months, she had grown so large that she would no longer fit into her accustomed place behind the stove and was forced to lie beside it. She was never given a name but was referred to in Gaelic as *cù mòr glas*, the big grey dog.

By the time she came into her first heat, she had grown to a tremendous height, and although her signs and her odour attracted many panting and highly aroused suitors, none was big enough to mount her and the frenzy of their disappointment and the longing of her unfulfilment were more than the man could stand. He went, so the story goes, to a place where he knew there was a big dog. A dog not as big as she was, but still a big dog, and he brought him home with him. And at the proper time he took the *cù mòr glas* and the big dog down to the sea where he knew there was a hollow in the rock which appeared only at low tide. He took some sacking to provide footing for the male dog and he placed the *cù mòr glas* in the hollow of the rock and knelt beside her and steadied her with his left arm under her throat and helped position the male dog above her and guided his blood-engorged penis. He was a man used to working with the breeding of animals, with the guiding of rams and bulls and stallions and often with the funky smell of animal semen heavy on his large and gentle hands.

The winter that followed was a cold one and ice formed on the sea and frequent squalls and blizzards obliterated the offshore islands and caused the people to stay near their fires much of the time, mending clothes and nets and harness and waiting for the change in season. The *cù mòr glas* grew heavier and even more large until there was hardly room for her around the stove or even under the table. And then one morning, when it seemed that spring was about to break, she was gone.

The man and even his family, who had become more involved than they cared to admit, waited for her but she did not come. And as the frenzy of spring wore on, they busied themselves with readying their land and their fishing gear and all of the things that so desperately required their attention. And then they were into summer and fall and winter and another spring which saw the birth of the man and his wife's twelfth child. And then it was summer again.

That summer the man and two of his teenaged sons were pulling their herring nets about two miles offshore when the wind began to blow off the land and the water began to roughen. They became afraid that they could not make it safely back to shore, so they pulled in behind one of the offshore islands, knowing that they would be sheltered there and planning to outwait the storm. As the prow of their boat approached the gravelly shore, they heard a sound above them, and looking up they saw the *cù mòr glas* silhouetted on the brow of the hill which was the small island's highest point.

"*M'eudal cù mòr glas*," shouted the man in his happiness – *m'eudal* meaning something like dear or darling; and as he shouted, he jumped over the side of his boat into the waist-deep water, struggling for footing on the rolling gravel as he waded eagerly and awkwardly towards her and the shore. At the same time, the *cù mòr glas* came hurtling down towards him in a shower of small rocks dislodged by her feet; and just as he was emerging from the water, she met him as she used to, rearing up on her hind legs and placing her huge front paws on his shoulders while extending her eager tongue.

The weight and speed of her momentum met him as he tried to hold his balance on the sloping angle and the water rolling gravel beneath his feet, and he staggered backwards and lost his footing and fell beneath her force. And in that instant again, as the story goes, there appeared over the brow of the hill six more huge grey dogs hurtling down towards the gravelled strand. They had never seen him before; and seeing him stretched prone beneath their mother, they misunderstood, like so many armies, the intention of their leader.

They fell upon him in a fury, slashing his face and tearing aside his lower jaw and ripping out his throat, crazed with blood-lust or duty or perhaps starvation. The *cù mòr glas* turned on them in her own savagery, slashing and snarling and, it seemed, crazed by their mistake; driving them bloodied and yelping before her, back over the brow of the hill where they vanished from sight but could still be heard screaming in the distance. It all took perhaps little more than a minute.

The man's two sons, who were still in the boat and had witnessed it all, ran sobbing through the salt water to where their mauled and mangled father lay; but there was little they could do other than hold his warm and bloodied hands for a few brief moments. Although his eyes "lived" for a small fraction of time, he could not speak to them because his face and throat had been torn away, and of course there was nothing they could do except to hold and be held tightly until that too slipped away and his eyes glazed over and they could no longer feel his hands holding theirs. The storm increased and they could not get home and so they were forced to spend the night huddled beside their father's body. They were afraid to try to carry the body to the rocking boat because he was so heavy and they were afraid that they might lose even what little of him remained and they were afraid also, huddled on the rocks, that the dogs might return. But they did not return at all and there was no sound from them, no sound at all, only the moaning of the wind and the washing of the water on the rocks.

In the morning they debated whether they should try to take his body with them or whether they should leave it and return in the company of older and wiser men. But they were afraid to leave it unattended and felt that the time needed to cover it with protective rocks would be better spent in trying to get across to their home shore. For a while they debated as to whether one should go in the boat and the other remain on the island, but each was afraid to be alone and so in the end they managed to drag and carry and almost float him towards the bobbing boat. They lay him facedown and covered him with what clothes there were and set off across the still-rolling sea. Those who waited on the shore missed the large presence of the man within the boat and some of them waded into the water and others rowed out in skiffs, attempting to hear the tearful messages called out across the rolling waves.

The *cù mòr glas* and her six young dogs were never seen again, or perhaps I should say they were never seen again in the same way. After some weeks, a group of men circled the island tentatively in their boats but they saw no sign. They went again and then again but found nothing. A year later, and grown much braver, they beached their boats and walked the island carefully, looking into the small sea caves and the hollows at the base of the wind-ripped trees, thinking perhaps that if they did not find the dogs, they might at least find their whitened bones; but again they discovered nothing.

The *cù mòr glas*, though, was supposed to be sighted here and there for a number of years. Seen on a hill in one region or silhouetted on a ridge in another or loping across the valleys or glens in the early morning or the shadowy evening. Always in the area of the half perceived. For a while she became rather like the Loch Ness Monster or the Sasquatch on a smaller scale. Seen but not recorded. Seen when there were no cameras. Seen but never taken.

The mystery of where she went became entangled with the mystery of whence she came. There was increased speculation about the handmade box in which she had been found and much theorizing as to the individual or individuals who might have left it. People went to look for the box but could not find it. It was felt she might have been part of a *buidseachd* or evil spell cast on the man by some mysterious enemy. But no one could go much farther than that. All of his caring for her was recounted over and over again and nobody missed any of the ironies.

What seemed literally known was that she had crossed the winter ice to have her pups and had been unable to get back.

No one could remember ever seeing her swim; and in the early months at least, she could not have taken her young pups with her.

The large and gentle man with the smell of animal semen often heavy on his hands was my great-great-great-grandfather, and it may be argued that he died because he was too good at breeding animals or that he cared too much about their fulfilment and well-being. He was no longer there for his own child of the spring who, in turn, became my great-great-grandfather, and he was perhaps too much there in the memory of his older sons who saw him fall beneath the ambiguous force of the *cù mòr glas*. The youngest boy in the boat was haunted and tormented by the awfulness of what he had seen. He would wake at night screaming that he had seen the *cù mòr glas a' bhàis,* the big grey dog of death, and his screams filled the house and the ears and minds of the listeners, bringing home again and again the consequences of their loss. One morning, after a night in which he saw the *cù mòr glas a' bhàis* so vividly that his sheets were drenched with sweat, he walked to the high cliff which faced the island and there he cut his throat with a fish knife and fell into the sea.

The other brother lived to be forty, but, again so the story goes, he found himself in a Glasgow pub one night, perhaps looking for answers, deep and sodden with the whiskey which had become his anaesthetic. In the half darkness he saw a large, grey-haired man sitting by himself against the wall and mumbled something to him. Some say he saw the *cù mòr glas a' bhàis* or uttered the name. And perhaps the man heard the phrase through ears equally affected by drink and felt he was being called a dog or a son of a bitch or something of that nature. They rose to meet one another and struggled outside into the cobblestoned passageway behind the pub where, most improbably, there were supposed to be six other large, grey-haired men who beat him to death on the cobblestones, smashing his bloodied head into the stone again and again before vanishing and leaving him to die with his face turned to the sky. The *cù mòr glas a' bhàis* had come again, said his family, as they tried to piece the tale together.

This is how the *cù mòr glas a' bhàis* came into our lives, and it is obvious that all of this happened a long, long time ago. Yet with succeeding generations it seemed the spectre had somehow come to stay and that it had become *ours* – not in the manner of an unwanted skeleton in the closet from a family's ancient past but more in the manner of something close to a genetic possibility. In the deaths of each generation, the grey dog was seen by some – by women who were to die in childbirth; by soldiers who went forth to the many wars but did not return; by those who went forth to feuds or dangerous love affairs; by those who answered mysterious midnight messages; by those who swerved on the highway to avoid the real or imagined grey dog and ended in masses of crumpled steel. And by one professional athlete who, in addition to his ritualized athletic superstitions, carried another fear or belief as well. Many of the man's descendants moved like careful hemophiliacs, fearing that they carried unwanted possibilities deep within them. And others, while they laughed, were like members of families in which there is a recurrence over the generations of repeated cancer or the diabetes which comes to those beyond middle age. The feeling of those who may say little to others but who may say often and quietly to themselves, "It has not happened to me," while adding always the cautionary "*yet*."

I am thinking all of this now as the October rain falls on the city of Toronto and the pleasant, white-clad nurses pad confidently in and out of my father's room. He lies quietly amidst the whiteness, his head and shoulders elevated so that he is in that hospital position of being neither quite prone nor yet sitting. His hair is white upon his pillow and he breathes softly and sometimes unevenly, although it is difficult ever to be sure.

My five grey-haired brothers and I take turns beside his bedside, holding his heavy hands in ours and feeling their response, hoping ambiguously that he will speak to us, although we know that it may tire him. And trying to read his life and ours into his eyes when they are open. He has been with us for a long time, well into our middle age. Unlike those boys in that boat of so long ago, we did not see him taken from us in our youth. And unlike their youngest brother who, in turn, became our great-great-grandfather, we did not grow into a world in which there was no father's touch. We have been lucky to have this large and gentle man so deep into our lives.

No one in this hospital has mentioned the *cù mòr glas a' bhàis.* Yet as my mother said ten years ago, before slipping into her own death as quietly as a grownup child who leaves or enters her parents' house in the early hours, "It is hard to *not* know what you do know."

Even those who are most sceptical, like my oldest brother who has driven here from Montreal, betray themselves by their nervous actions. "I avoided the Greyhound bus stations in both Montreal and Toronto," he smiled upon his arrival, and then added, "Just in case."

He did not realize how ill our father was and has smiled little since then. I watch him turning the diamond ring upon his finger, knowing that he hopes he will not hear the Gaelic phrase he knows too well. Not having the luxury, as he once said, of some who live in Montreal and are able to pretend they do not understand the "other" language. You cannot *not* know what you do know.

Sitting here, taking turns holding the hands of the man who gave us life, we are afraid for him and for ourselves. We are afraid of what he may see and we are afraid to hear the phrase born of the vision. We are aware that it may become confused with what the doctors call "the will to live" and we are aware that some beliefs are what others would dismiss as "garbage." We are aware that there are men who believe the earth is flat and that the birds bring forth the sun.

Bound here in our own peculiar mortality, we do not wish to see or see others see that which signifies life's demise. We do not want to hear the voice of our father, as did those other sons, calling down his own particular death upon him.

We would shut our eyes and plug our ears, even as we know such actions to be of no avail. Open still and fearful to the grey hair rising on our necks if and when we hear the scrabble of the paws and the scratching at the door.

Vision

I DON'T REMEMBER when I first heard the story but I remember the first time that I heard it and remembered it. By that I mean the first time it made an impression on me and more or less became *mine*; sort of went into me the way such things do, went into me in such a way that I knew it would not leave again but would remain there forever. Something like when you cut your hand with a knife by accident, and even as you're trying to staunch the blood flowing out of the wound, you know the wound will never really heal totally and your hand will never look quite the same again. You can imagine the scar tissue that will form and be a different colour and texture from the rest of your skin. You know this even as you are trying to stop the blood and trying to squeeze the separated edges of skin together once more. Like trying to squeeze together the separated banks of a small and newly discovered river so that the stream will be subterranean once again. It is something like that, although you know in one case the future scar will be forever on the outside while the memory will remain forever deep within.

Anyway, on this day we were about a mile and a half offshore but heading home on the last day of the lobster season. We could see the trucks of the New Brunswick buyers waiting for us on the wharf and because it was a sunny day, light reflected and glinted off the chrome trim and bumpers of the waiting trucks and off their gleaming rooftops as well. It was the last day of June and the time was early afternoon and I was seventeen.

My father was in good spirits because the season was over and we had done reasonably well and we were bringing in most of our gear intact. And there seemed no further need to rush.

The sea was almost calm, although there was a light breeze at our backs and we throttled down our engine because there really was no reason to hurry into the wharf for the last and final time. I was in the stern of the boat steadying the piled lobster traps which we had recently raised from the bottom of the sea. Some of them still gleamed with droplets of salt water and streamers of seaweed dangled from their lathes. In the crates beside my feet the mottled blue-green lobsters moved and rustled quietly, snapping their tails as they slid over one another with that peculiar dry/wet sound of shell and claws over shell and claws. Their hammer claws had been pegged and fastened shut with rubber bands so they would not mutilate each other and so decrease their value.

"Put some of those in a sack for ourselves," said my father, turning his head back over his right shoulder as he spoke. He was standing ahead of me, facing the land and urinating over the side. His water fell into the sea and vanished into the rolling swell of the boat's slow passage.

"Put them in the back there," he said, "behind the bait bucket, and throw our oilers over them. They will want everything we've got, and what they won't see won't hurt them. Put in some markets too, not just canners."

I took a sack and began to pick some lobsters out of the crate, grasping them at the end of their body shells or by the ends of their tails and being careful not to get my fingers snapped. For even with their hammer claws banded shut there was still a certain danger.

"How many do you want?" I asked.

"Oh," he said, turning with a smile and running his hand

along the front of his trousers to make sure his fly was closed, "as many as you want. Use your own good judgement."

We did not often take home lobsters for ourselves because they were so expensive and we needed the money they would bring. And the buyers wanted them with a desperation almost bordering on frenzy. Perhaps even now as I bent over the crate they were watching from the wharf with binoculars to see if any were being concealed. My father stood casually in front of me, once more facing the land and shielding my movements with his body. The boat followed its set course, its keel cutting the blue-green water and turning it temporarily into white.

There was a time long ago when the lobsters were not thought to be so valuable. Probably because the markets of the larger world had not yet been discovered or were so far away. People then ate all they wanted of them and even used them for fertilizer on their fields. And those who did eat them did not consider them to be a delicacy. There is a quoted story from the time which states that in the schools you could always identify the children of the poor because they were the ones with lobster in their sandwiches. The well-to-do were able to afford bologna.

With the establishment of the New England market, things changed. Lobster factories were set up along the coast for the canning of the lobsters at a time before good land transportation and refrigeration became common. In May and June and into July the girls in white caps and smocks packed the lobster meat into burnished cans before they were steam sealed. And the men in the smack boats brought the catches to the rickety piers which were built on piles and jutted out into the sea.

My father's mother was one of the girls, and her job was taking the black vein out of the meat of the lobster's tail before the tail was coiled around the inside of the can. At home they ate the black vein along with the rest of the meat, but the supervisors at the factory said it was unsightly. My father's father was one of the young men standing ready in the smack

boat, wearing his cap at a jaunty angle and uttering witty say-
ings and singing little songs in Gaelic to the girls who stood
above him on the wharf. All of this was of course a long time
ago and I am just trying to recreate the scene.

On the day of the remembered story, though, the sea was
almost serene as I placed the lobsters in the sack and prepared
to hide them behind the bait bucket and under our oilers in
the stern of the boat. Before we secreted the sack, we leaned
over the side and scooped up water in the bailing bucket and
soaked the sack to insure the health and life of the lobsters kept
within. The wet sack moved and clacked with the shape and
sound of the lobsters and it reminded me vaguely of sacks of
kittens which were being taken to be drowned. You could see
the movement but not the individuals.

My father straightened from his last dip over the side and
passed the dripping bucket carefully to me. He steadied himself with his left hand on the gunwale and then seated himself
on the thwart and faced towards the north. I gave the lobsters
another soaking and moved to place them behind the bait
bucket. There was still some bait remaining but we would not
have need of it anymore so I threw it over the side. The pieces
of blue-grey mackerel turned and revolved before I lost sight
of them within the water. The day before yesterday we had
taken these same mackerel out of the same sea. We used nets
for the spring mackerel because they were blind and could not
see to take a baited hook; but in the fall when they returned,
the scales had fallen from their eyes and they would lunge at
almost anything thrown before them. Even bits of other
mackerel ground up and mixed with salt. Mackerel are a
windward fish and always swim against the wind. If the wind
is off the land, they swim towards the shore and perhaps the
waiting nets; but if the wind blows in the opposite direction,
they face out to sea and go so far out some years that we miss
them altogether.

I put the empty bait bucket in front of the sack of lobsters and placed an empty crate upside down and at an angle over them so that their movements would not be noticeable. And I casually threw our oilers over them as well.

Ahead of us on the land and to the north of the wharf with its waiting trucks was the mile-long sandy beach cut by the river which acted as an erratic boundary between the fishing grounds of ourselves and our neighbours, the MacAllesters. We had traditionally fished to the right of the river and they to the left, and apparently for many years it was constant in its estuary. But in recent years the river mouth, because of the force of storms and tides and the buildup of sand, had become undependable as a visual guide. The shifting was especially affected by the ravages of the winter storms, and some springs the river might empty almost a mile to the north or the south of its previous point of entry. This had caused a tension between ourselves and the MacAllesters because, although we traditionally went to the same grounds, the boundary was no longer fixed and we had fallen into accusations and counter-accusations; sometimes using the actual river when it suited our purpose, and when it did not, using an earlier and imaginary river which we could no longer see.

The MacAllesters' boat was going in ahead of us now and I waved to Kenneth MacAllester, who had become a rather lukewarm friend because of the tension between our families. He was the same age as I and he waved back, although the other two men in the boat did not.

At an earlier time when Kenneth MacAllester and I were friends and in about grade six he told me a story while we were walking home from school in the spring. He told me that his grandmother was descended from a man in Scotland who possessed *Da Shealladh*, two sights or the second sight, and that by looking through a hole in a magical white stone he could see distant contemporary events as well as those of the future. Nearly all of his visions came true. His name was either Munro or MacKenzie and his first name was Kenneth and the eye he placed to the stone for his visions was *cam* or blind in the sense of ordinary sight. He was a favourite of the powerful man for whom he worked but he and the man's wife were jealous and disliked each other. Once when the powerful man was in Paris there was a big party on his estate. In one version "the prophet" commented rather unwisely on the paternity of some of the children present. In another version the man's wife asked him mockingly if he could "see" her husband in Paris but he refused. However, she insisted. Putting the stone to his eye he told her that her husband was enjoying himself rather too much with ladies in Paris and had little thought of her. Enraged and embarrassed, she ordered him to be burned in a barrel of tar into which spikes had been driven from the outside. In one version the execution took place right away but in another it did not take place until some days later. In the second version the man was returning home when he heard the news and saw the black smoke rising. He spurred his horse at utmost speed towards the point where he saw the billowing smoke and called out in an attempt to stop the burning and save his friend; but his horse died beneath him, and though he ran the rest of the way, he arrived too late for any salvation.

Before the prophet died he hurled his white stone as far as he could out into the lake and told the lady that the family would come to an end years hence. And he told her that it would end when there was a deaf-and-dumb father who would outlive his four sons and then all their lands would pass into the hands of strangers. Generations later the deaf-and-dumb father was apparently a fine, good man who was helpless in the face of the prophecy he knew too much about and which he saw unfolding around him with the death of each of his four loved sons. Unable again to offer any salvation.

I thought it was a tremendous story at the time, and Kenneth picked up a white stone from the roadside and held it to his eye to see if "prophecy" would work for him.

"I guess I really wouldn't want it to work," he said with a

laugh. "I wouldn't want to be blind," and he threw the stone away. At that time he planned on joining the Air Force and flying towards the sun and being able to see over the tops of mountains and across the sea.

When we got to his house we were still talking about the story and his mother cautioned us not to laugh at such things. She went and found a poem by Sir Walter Scott, which she read aloud to us. We did not pay much attention to it but I remember the lines which referred to the father and his four doomed sons:

> *Thy sons rose around thee in light and in love*
> *All a father could hope, all a friend could approve;*
> *What 'vails it the tale of thy sorrows to tell?*
> *In the springtime of youth and of promise they fell!*

Now, as I said, the MacAllesters' boat was going in ahead of us, loaded down with its final catch and with its stern and washboard piled high with traps. We had no great wish to talk to the MacAllesters at the wharf and there were other boats ahead of us as well. They would unload their catches first and pile their traps upon the wharf and it would be some time before we would find a place to dock. My father cut our engine. There was no need to rush.

"Do you see Canna over there?" he asked, pointing to the north where he was facing. "Do you see the point of Canna?"

"Yes," I said, "I see it. There it is."

There was nothing very unusual about seeing the point of Canna. It was always visible except on the foggiest days or when there was rain or perhaps snow. It was twenty miles away by boat and on the duller days it reached out low and blue like the foot of a giant's boot extended into the sea. On sunny days like this one it sparkled in a distant green. The clearings of the old farms were visible and above them the line of the encroaching trees, the spruce and fir of a darker green. Here and there the white houses stood out and even the grey and weather-beaten barns. It was called after the Hebridean island of Canna, "the green island" where most of its original settlers were born. It was the birthplace of my grandmother who was one of the girls in the white smocks at the Canna lobster factory in that long-ago time.

"It was about this time of year," said my father, "that your Uncle Angus and I went by ourselves to visit our grandmother at the point of Canna. We were eleven at the time and had been asking our parents for weeks to let us go. They seemed reluctant to give us any answer and all they would say was 'We will see' or 'Wait and see.' We wanted to go on the smack boat when it was making its final run of the season. We wanted to go with the men on the smack who were buying lobsters and they would set us ashore at the wharf of Canna point and we would walk the mile to our grandmother's house. We had never gone there by ourselves before. We could hardly remember being there because if you went by land you had to travel by horse and buggy and it was a long way. First you had to go inland to the main road and drive about twenty miles and then come back down towards the shore. It was about twice as far by land as it was by sea and our parents went about once a year. Usually by themselves as there was not enough room for others in the buggy. If we did not get to go on the smack, we were afraid that we would not get to go at all. 'Wait and see' was all they said."

It seemed strange to me, as my father spoke, to think of Canna as far away. By that time it took perhaps three-quarters of an hour by car, even though the final section of the road was often muddy and dangerous enough in the wet months of spring and fall and often blocked by snow in the winter. Still, it was not hard to get there if you really wanted to, and so the old letters from Canna which I discovered in the upstairs attic seemed quite strange and from another distant time. It seemed hard to believe that people only twenty miles away would write letters to one another and only visit once a year.

But at that time the distance was hard to negotiate and there were no telephones.

My father and his brother Angus were twins and they had been named after their grandfathers so their names were Angus and Alex. It was common for parents to name their first children after their own parents and it seemed that almost all of the men were called Angus or Alex. In the early years of the century the Syrian and Lebanese pedlars who walked the muddy country roads beneath their heavy backpacks sometimes called themselves Angus or Alex so that they would sound more familiar to their potential customers. The pedlars, like the Gaelic-speaking people in the houses which they visited, had very little English, so anything that aided communication was helpful. Sometimes they unfolded their bolts of cloth and displayed their shining needles before admirers who were unable to afford them, and sometimes sensing the situation they would leave the goods behind. Later, if money became available, the people would say, "Put aside what we owe Angus and Alex in the sugar bowl so that we can pay them when they come."

Sometimes the pedlars would carry letters from one community to the other, to and from the families of the different Anguses and Alexes strung out along the coast. Distinguishing the different families, although their names were much the same, and delivering letters which they could not read.

My father and his brother continued to pester their parents who continued to say "Wait and see," and then one day they went to visit their father's mother who lived in a house quite close to theirs. After they had finished the lunch she had given them, she offered to "read" their teacups and to tell them of the future events revealed in the tea leaves at the bottoms of their cups: "You are going on a journey," she said, peering into the cups as she turned them in her hands. "You are going to cross water. And to take food with you. You will meet a mysterious woman who has dark hair. She will be quite close to you.

And …" she said, turning the cups in her hands to better see the formation of the leaves, "and … oh … oh … oh."

"What?" they asked. "What?"

"Oh, that's enough for today," she said. "You had better be getting home or they will be worrying about you."

They ran home and burst into their parents' kitchen. "We are going on a trip to Canna," they said. "Grandma told us. She saw it in the tea leaves. She read it in our cups. We are going to take a lunch. We are going across the water. She *said* we were going."

The morning they left they were dressed in their best clothes and waiting at the wharf long before the smack was due, clutching their lunches in their hands. It was sunny when the boat left the wharf but as they proceeded along the coast it became cloudy and then it began to rain. The trip seemed long in the rain and the men told them to go into the boat's cabin where they would be dry and where they could eat their lunch. The first part of the trip seemed to be spoiled by rain.

It was raining heavily when the boat approached the wharf at Canna point. It was almost impossible to see the figures on the wharf or to distinguish them as they moved about in their heavy oil slickers. The lobster buyers were in a hurry, as were the wet men impatiently waiting for them in the rain.

"Do you know where you're going?" said the men in the smack to their young passengers.

"Yes," they said, although they were not quite sure because the rain obscured the landmarks that they thought they would remember.

"Here," said the men in the smack, handing them two men's oil slickers from the boat's cabin. "Wear these to help keep you dry. You can give them back to us sometime."

They climbed up the iron ladder towards the wharf's cap and the busy men reached their hands down to help and pull them up.

Because the men were busy and because of the rain no one

on the wharf asked them where they were going and they were too shy and too proud to ask. So they turned the cuffs of the oil slickers back over their wrists and began to walk up the muddy road from the wharf. They were still trying to keep their best clothes clean and pick their spots carefully, placing their good shoes where there were fairly dry spots and avoiding the puddles and little rivulets which rolled the small stones along in their course. The oil slickers were so long that the bottoms of them dragged on the muddy road and sometimes they lifted them up in the way that older ladies might lift the hems of their skirts when stepping over a puddle or some other obstacle in the roadway. When they lifted them, the muddy bottoms rubbed against their good trousers so they let them fall again. Then their shoes were almost invisible and they could hear and feel the tails of the coats dragging behind them as they walked. They were wet and miserable inside the long coats as well as undistinguishable to anyone who might see the small forms in the long coats walking along the road.

After they had walked for half a mile they were overtaken by an old man in a buggy who stopped and offered them a ride. He too was covered in an oil coat and his cap was pulled down almost to his nose. When he stopped to pick them up, the steam rose from his horse as they clambered into the wagon beside him. He spoke to them in Gaelic and asked them their names and where they were from and where they were going.

"To see our grandmother," they said.

"Your grandmother?" he asked.

"Yes," they said. "Our grandmother."

"Oh," he said. "Your grandmother, are you sure?"

"Of course," they said, becoming a bit annoyed. For although they were more uncertain than they cared to admit, they did not want to appear so.

"Oh," he said, "all right then. Would you like some pepper-mints?" And he reached deeply into a pocket beneath his oil coat and brought out a brown paper bag full of peppermints.

Even as he passed the bag to them, the raindrops pelted upon it and it became soggy and began to darken in deterioration.

"Oh," he said, "you may as well keep all of them. I got a whole lot more of them for the store. They just came in on the boat." He motioned to some metal containers in the back of the buggy.

"Are you going to spend the night with your grandmother?" he asked.

"Yes," they said.

"Oh," he answered, pulling on the reins and turning the horse into the laneway of a yard.

He drove them to the door of the house and helped them down from the buggy while his horse stomped its impatient hooves in the mud and tossed its head in the rain.

"Would you like me to go in with you?" he asked.

"No," they said, impatient for him to be gone and out of sight.

"All right," he said and spoke to his uneasy horse which began to trot down the laneway, the buggy wheels throwing hissing jets of mud and water behind them.

They hesitated for a while outside the doorway of the house, waiting for the man to go out of sight and feeling ridiculous for standing in the rain. But halfway down the lane he stopped and looked back. And then he stood up in the buggy and shouted to them and made a "go-forward" gesture with his hand towards the house. They opened the door then and went in because they felt embarrassed and did not want to admit that he had brought them to the wrong house.

When they went in, they found themselves in the middle of a combined porch and entranceway which was cluttered with an odd collection of household and farming utensils. Baking pans and jars and sealers and chamber pots and old milk pails and rakes and hoes and hayforks and bits of wire and lengths of chain. There was very little light, and in the gloom something started up from their feet and bounced against their legs and then into a collection of jars and pails, causing a crashing cacophony of sound. It was a half-grown lamb and it bleated as it bounded towards the main door, dropping bits of manure behind it. In the same instant and in response to the sound, the main door opened and the lamb leaped through it and into the house.

Framed in the doorway was a tall old woman clad in layers of clothing, even though it was summer, and wearing wire-framed glasses. On either side of her were two black dogs. They were like collies, although they had no white markings. They growled softly but deep within their throats and the fur on the back of their necks rose and they raised their upper lips to reveal their gleaming teeth. They were poised on the tips of their paws and their eyes seemed to burn in the gloom. She lowered a hand to each of their heads but did not say anything. Everyone seemed to stare straight ahead. The boys would have run away but they were afraid that if they moved, the dogs would be upon them, so they stayed where they were as still as could be. The only sound was the tense growling of the dogs. "*Cò a th'ann?*" she said in Gaelic. "Who's there?"

The boys did not know what to say because all the possible answers seemed so complicated. They moved their feet uneasily, which caused the dogs to each take two steps forward as if they were part of some rehearsed choreography. "*Cò a th'ann?*" she said, repeating the question. "Who's there?"

"We're from Kintail," they said finally. "Our names are Alex and Angus. We're trying to find our grandmother's house. We came on the smack boat."

"Oh," she said. "How old are you?"

"Eleven," they said. "Both of us. We're twins."

"Oh," she said. "Both of you. I have relatives in Kintail. Come in."

They were still afraid and the dogs remained poised, snarling softly with their delicate, dangerous lips flickering above the whiteness of their teeth.

"All right," they said. "We'll come in, but just for a minute. We can't stay long."

Only then did she speak to the dogs. "Go and lie under the table and be quiet," she said. Immediately they relaxed and vanished behind her into the house.

"Did you know these dogs were twins?" she asked.

"No," they said. "We didn't."

"Well," she said. "They are."

Inside the house they sat on the first chairs that they could find and moved them as close to the door as possible. The room that they were in was a primitive kitchen and much of its floor was cluttered with objects not unlike the porch except that the objects were smaller – knives and forks and spoons and the remains of broken cups and saucers. There was a half-completed partition between the kitchen and what might have been a living room or dining room. The upright studs of the partition were firmly in place and someone had nailed wainscotting on either side of them but it only extended half-way to the ceiling. It was difficult to tell if the partition had been left incomplete or if it was gradually being lowered. The space between the walls of the partition was filled with cats. They pulled themselves up by their paws and looked curiously at the visitors and then jumped back down into the space. From the space between the incompleted walls the visitors could hear the mewing of newborn kittens. Other cats were everywhere. They were on the table, licking what dishes there were, and on the backs of the chairs and in and out of a cavern beneath an old couch. Sometimes they leaped over the half-completed partition and vanished into the next room. Sometimes they snarled at one another and feinted with the paws. In one corner a large tiger-striped tomcat was energetically breeding a small grey female flattened out beneath him. Other tentative males circled the breeding pair, growling deeply within their throats. The tiger cat would interrupt his movements from time to time to snarl at them and keep them at bay.

The female's nose was pressed against the floor and her ears flattened down against her head. Sometimes he held the fur at the back of her neck within his teeth.

The two black dogs lay under the table and seemed oblivious to the cats. The lamb stood watchfully behind the stove. Everything in the house was extremely dirty – spilled milk and cat hair and unwashed and broken dishes. The old woman wore men's rubber boots upon her feet and her clothing seemed to consist of layers of petticoats and skirts and dresses and sweaters upon sweaters. All of it was very dirty and covered with stains of spilled tea and food remnants and spattered grease. Her hands seemed brown and her fingernails were long and there was a half inch of black grime under each of them. She raised her hands to touch her glasses and they noticed that the outside lenses were smeared and filthy as well. It was then that they realized that she was blind and that the glasses served no useful purpose. They became even more uncertain and frightened than they were before.

"Which one of you is Alex?" she asked, and he raised his hand as if answering a question at school before realizing that she could not see him.

"I am," he answered then, and she turned her face in his direction.

"I have a long association with that name," she said, and they were surprised at her use of a word like "association."

Because of the rain the day seemed to darken early and they could see the fading light through the grimy windows. They wondered for a moment why she did not light a lamp until they realized that there was none and that to her it made no difference.

"I will make you a lunch," she said. "Don't move."

She went to the partial partition and ripped the top board off with her strong brown hands and then she leaned it against the partition and stomped on it with her rubber-booted foot. It splintered and she repeated the action, feeling about the floor for the lengths of splintered wood. She gathered them up and went to the stove and, after removing the lids, began to feed them into the fire. She moved the kettle over the crackling flame.

She began to feel about the cupboards for food, brushing away the insistent cats which crowded about her hands. She found two biscuits in a tin and placed them on plates which she put into the cupboard so the cats would not devour them. She put her hand into a tea tin and took a handful of tea which she placed in the teapot and then she poured the hot water in as well. She found some milk in a dirty pitcher and feeling for the cups she splashed some of it into each.

Then she took the teapot and began to pour the tea. She turned her back to them but as she poured they could see her quickly dip her long brown finger with the half inch of grimy fingernail quickly into each cup. They realized she was doing it because she had no other way of knowing when the cups were full but their stomachs revolved and they feared they might throw up.

She brought them a cup of tea each and retrieved the biscuits from the cupboard and passed the plates to them. They sat holding the offerings on their laps while she faced them. Although they realized she could not see them, they still felt that she was watching them. They looked at the tea and the biscuits with the cat hair and did not know what to do. After a while they began to make slurping sounds with their lips.

"Well, we will have to be on our way," they said. Carefully they bent forward and placed the still-full teacups under their chairs and the biscuits in their pockets.

"Do you know where you are going?" she asked.

"Yes," they said with determination.

"Can you see your way in the dark?"

"Yes," they said again with equal determination.

"We will meet again?" she said, raising her voice to form a question.

"Yes," they said.

"Some are more loyal than others," she said. "Remember that."

They hurried down the laneway, surprised to find that it was not so dark outside as it seemed within the blind woman's house. When they got to the main road, they followed it in the direction that led away from the wharf and it seemed that in a short time they could make out the buildings of their original intended destination.

It was still raining as they entered the laneway to the buildings, and by this time it was indeed quite dark. The laneway ended at the door of the barn and the house was some yards farther. The barn door was open and they stepped inside for a moment to compose themselves. It was very quiet within the barn for all of the animals were away in their summer pastures. They hesitated for a moment in the first stall and then they were aware of a rhythm of sound coming from the next area, the threshing floor. They opened the small connecting door and stepped inside and waited for their eyes to adjust to the gloom. And then in the farthest corner they noticed a lantern turned to its lowest and hanging on a nail. And beyond it they could make out the shape of a man. He was tall and wore rubber boots and bib overalls and had a tweed cap pulled down upon his head. He was facing the south wall of the barn but was sideways to them and presented a profile. He was rhythmically rocking from his heels to the balls of his feet and thrusting his hips back and forth and moaning and talking to himself in Gaelic. But it did not seem that he was talking to himself but to someone of the opposite sex who was not there. The front of his overalls was open and he had a hold of himself in his right hand which he moved to the rhythm of his rocking body.

They did not know what to do. They did not recognize the man and they were terrified that he might turn and see them and they were afraid that if they tried to make a retreat they might cause a sound which would betray their presence. At home they slept upstairs while their parents slept below in a private room ("to keep an eye on the fire," their parents said); and although they were becoming curious about sex, they did not know a great deal about it. They had seen the mating of animals, such as the earlier cats, but they had never seen a fully aroused grown man before, although they recognized some of the words he was moaning to himself and his imaginary partner. Suddenly with a groan he slumped forward as the grey jets of seed spurted onto the south wall of the barn and down to the dry and dusty hay before his feet. He placed his left arm against the wall and rested his forehead against it. They stepped back quietly through the little door and then out of the barn and then they walked rapidly but on their tiptoes through the rain towards the house.

When they entered the porch and the screen door slammed behind them, they heard a voice from within the kitchen. It was harsh and angry and seemed to be cursing, and then the door flew open and they were face to face with their grandmother. At first she did not recognize them in their long coats and her face remained suspicious and angry, but then her expression changed and she came forward to hug them.

"Angus and Alex," she said. "What a surprise!" Looking over their shoulders, she said, "Are you alone? Did you come by yourselves?" And then, "Why didn't you tell us you were coming? We would have gone to meet you."

It had never entered their minds that their arrival would be such a surprise. They had been thinking of the trip with such intensity that in spite of the day's happenings they still somehow assumed that everyone knew they were coming.

"Well, come in, come in," she said, "and take those wet clothes off. How did you say you came again? And are you just arriving now?"

They told her they had come on the smack and of their walk and the ride with the man who had the peppermints and of their visit to the blind woman, but they omitted the part about the man in the barn. She listened intently as she moved about the kitchen, hanging up their coats and setting the teapot on the stove. She asked for a description of the man with the peppermints and they told her he said he owned a store, and then she asked them how the blind woman was. They told her of the tea she had served them which they had left and she said, "Poor soul!"

And then the screen door banged again and a heavy foot was heard in the porch, and then in through the kitchen door walked the man they had seen in the barn.

"Your grandchildren are here to see you," she said with an icy edge to her voice. "They came on the smack from Kintail."

He stood blinking and swaying in the light, trying to focus his eyes upon them. They realized then that he was quite drunk and having difficulty comprehending. His eyes were red-rimmed and bloodshot and a white stubble speckled with black indicated that he had not shaved for a number of days. He swayed back and forth, looking at them carefully and trying to see who they really were. They could not help looking at the front of his overalls to see if there were flecks of semen, but he had been out in the rain and all of his clothing was splattered with moisture.

"Oh," he said, as if a veil had been lifted from his eyes. "Oh," he said. "I love you. I love you." And he came forward and hugged each of them and kissed them on the cheek. They could smell the sourness of his breath and feel the rasping scratch of his stubble on their faces.

"Well," he said, turning on his heel, "I am going upstairs to rest for awhile. I have been out in the barn and have been busier than you might think. But I will be back down later." And then he kicked off his boots, steadying himself with one hand on a kitchen chair, and swayed upstairs.

The visitors were shocked that they had not recognized their grandfather. When he came to visit them perhaps once a year, he was always splendid and handsome in his blue serge suit, with a gold watch chain linked across the expansiveness of his vest. And with his pockets filled with peppermints. And when they visited in the company of their parents, he had always been gracious and clear-headed and well attired.

When they could no longer hear his footsteps, their grandmother again began to talk to them, asking them questions, inquiring of their parents and of their school work as she busied herself about the stove and began to set the table.

Later he came back downstairs and they all sat around the table. He had changed his clothes and his face was covered with bleeding knicks because he had tried to shave. The meal was uncomfortable as he knocked over his water glass and dropped his food on his lap. The visitors were exhausted as he was and only their grandmother seemed in control. He went back upstairs as soon as the meal was finished, saying, "Tomorrow will be a better day," and their grandmother suggested that they go to bed soon after.

"We are all tired," she said. "He will be all right tomorrow. He tried to shave in honour of your coming. I will talk to him myself. We are glad that you have come."

They slept together under a mountain of quilts and in a room next to their grandparents. Before they went to sleep they could hear them talking in Gaelic, and the next thing they remembered was waking in the morning. Their grandparents were standing near their bed and the sun was shining through the window. Each of their grandparents held a tray containing porridge and sugar and milk and tea and butter. They were both rather formally dressed and like the grandparents they thought they knew. The drunk moaning man in the barn was like a dream they wished they had not had.

When they got up to put on their clothes they discovered bits of the blind woman's biscuits still in their pockets, and when they went outside they threw them behind the barn.

They stayed a week at Canna and all during that time the

sun shone and the days were golden. They went visiting with their grandfather in his buggy – visiting women in houses and sometimes standing in barns with men. One day they visited the store and had trouble identifying the man behind the counter with the one who had offered them the ride and the peppermints. He seemed equally surprised when he recognized them and said to their grandfather, "I'm sorry if I made a mistake."

During their week in Canna they noticed small differences in the way of doing things. The people of Canna tied their horses with ropes around their necks instead of with halters. They laid out their gardens in beds instead of in rows and they grew a particular type of strawberry whose fruit grew far from the original root. When they drew water from their wells they threw away the first dipperful and the water itself had a slightly different taste. They set their tables for breakfast before retiring for the night. They bowed or curtsied to the new moon and in the Church of St. Columba the women sat on one side of the aisle and the men on the other.

The Church of St. Columba, said their grandfather, was called after the original chapel on the island of Canna. St. Columba of Colum Cille was a brilliant, dedicated missionary in Ireland and he possessed *Da Shealladh,* the second sight, and used a stone to "see" his visions. He was also a lover of beauty and very strong-willed. Once, continued their grandfather, he copied a religious manuscript without permission but believed the copy was rightfully his. The High King of Ireland who was asked to judge the dispute ruled against Colum Cille, saying, "To every cow its calf and to every book its copy." Later the High King of Ireland also executed a young man who had sought sanctuary under the protection of Colum Cille. Enraged at what he perceived as injustice and bad judgement, Colum Cille told the High King he would lead his relations and clansmen against him in battle. On the eve of the battle, as they prayed and fasted, the archangel Michael appeared to

Colum Cille in a vision. The angel told him that God would answer his prayers and allow him to win the battle but that He was not pleased with him for praying for such a worldly request and that he should exile himself from Ireland and never see the country anymore or its people or partake of its food and drink except on his outward journey. The forces of Colum Cille won the battle and inflicted losses of three thousand men, and perhaps he could have been the King of Ireland but he obeyed the vision. Some said he left also to do penance for the three thousand lives he had cost. In a small boat and with a few followers who were his relatives, he crossed the sea to the small islands of Scotland and spent the last thirty-four years of his life establishing monasteries and chapels and travelling among the people. Working as a missionary, making predictions, seeing visions and changing forever that region of the world. Leaving Ireland, he said:

> *There is a grey eye*
> *Looking back on Ireland,*
> *That will never see again*
> *Her men or her women.*
>
> *Early and late my lamentation,*
> *Alas, the journey I am making;*
> *This will be my secret bye-name*
> *"Back turned on Ireland."*

"Did he ever go back?" they asked.

"Once," said their grandfather, "the poets of Ireland were in danger of being banned and he crossed the sea from Scotland to speak on their behalf. But when he came, he came blindfolded so that he could not see the country or its people."

"Did you know him?" they asked. "Did you ever see him?"

"That was a very long time ago," he laughed. "Over thirteen hundred years ago. But, yes, sometimes I feel I know him and I think I see him as well. This church, as I said, is called after the chapel he established on Canna. That chapel is fallen a long time ago too and all of the people gone, and the well beside the chapel filled up with rocks and the Celtic crosses of their graveyards smashed down and used for the building of roads. But sometimes I imagine I still see them," he said, looking towards the ocean and across it as if he could see the "green island" and its people. "I see them going about their rituals: riding their horses on Michaelmas and carrying the bodies of their dead round towards the sun. And courting and getting married. Almost all of the people on Canna got married before they were twenty. They considered it unlucky to be either a single man or woman so there were very few single people among them. Perhaps they also found it difficult to wait," he added with a smile, "and that is why their population rose so rapidly. Anyway, all gone."

"You mean dead?" they asked.

"Well, some of them, yes," he said, "but I mean gone from there, scattered all over the world. But some of us are here. That is why this place is called Canna and we carry certain things within us. Sometimes there are things within us which we do not know or fully understand and sometimes it is hard to stamp out what you can't see. It is good that you are here for this while."

Towards the end of the week they learned that there was a government boat checking lighthouses along the coast. It would stop at the point of Canna and later, on its southern journey, also at Kintail. It was an excellent chance for them to get home and it was decided that they should take it. The night before they left, their grandparents served them a splendid dinner with a white tablecloth and candles.

As they prepared to leave on the following morning, the rain began to fall. Their grandmother gave them some packages to deliver to their mother and also a letter and packed a lunch with lobster sandwiches for them. She hugged and kissed them as they were leaving and said, "Thank you for coming. It was good to have you here and it made us feel better about ourselves." She looked at her husband and he nodded.

They climbed into their grandfather's buggy as the rain fell upon them and carefully placed their packages beneath the seat. On the road down to the wharf they passed the lane to the blind woman's house. She was near the roadway with the two black dogs. She was wearing her men's rubber boots and a large kerchief and a heavy rubber raincoat. When she heard the buggy approaching, she called out, "*Cò a th'ann? Cò a th'ann?* Who's there? Who's there?"

But their grandfather said nothing.

"Who's there?" she called. "Who's there? Who's there?"

The rain fell upon her streaked and empty glasses and down her face and along her coat and her strong protruding hands with their grimy fingernails.

"Don't say anything," said their grandfather under his breath. "I don't want her to know you're here."

As the horse approached, she continued to call but none of them said anything. Above the regular hoofbeats of the horse her voice seemed to rise through the falling rain, causing a tension within all of them as they tried to pretend they could not hear her.

"*Cò a th'ann?*" she called. "Who's there? Who's there?"

They lowered their heads as if she could see them. But when they were exactly opposite her, their grandfather could not stand it any longer and suddenly reined in the horse.

"*Cò a th'ann?*" she called. "Who's there?"

"'*Se mi-fhìn,*" he answered quietly. "It's myself!"

She began to curse him in Gaelic and he became embarrassed.

"Do you understand what she's saying?" he said to them.

They were uncertain. "Some of it," they said.

"Here," he said, "hold the horse," and he passed the reins to them. He took the buggy whip out of its socket as he descended from the buggy and they were uncertain about that too until they realized he was taking it to protect himself from the dogs who came snarling towards him but kept their distance because of the whip. He began to talk to the blind woman in Gaelic and they both walked away from the buggy along the laneway to her house until they were out of earshot. The dogs lay down on the wet roadway and watched and listened carefully.

The visitors could not hear the conversation, only the rising and falling of the two voices through the descending rain. When their grandfather returned, he seemed upset and took the reins from them and spoke to the horse immediately.

"God help me," he said softly and almost to himself, "but I could not pass her by."

There was water running down his face and they thought for a moment he might be crying; but just as when they had looked for the semen on his overalls a week earlier, they could not tell because of the rain.

The blind woman stood in the laneway facing them as they moved off along the road. It was one of those situations which almost automatically calls for waving but even as they began to raise their hands they remembered her blindness and realized it was no use. She stood as if watching them for a long time and then, perhaps when she could no longer hear the sound of the horse and buggy, she turned and walked with the two dogs back towards her house.

"Do you know her well?" they asked.

"Oh," said their grandfather, as if being called back from another time and place, "yes, I do know her quite well and since a long, long time."

Their grandfather waited with them on the wharf for the coming of the government boat, but it was late. When it finally arrived, the men said they would not be long checking the lighthouse and told them to go into the boat to wait. They said their good-byes then and their grandfather turned his wet and impatient horse towards home.

Although the wait was not supposed to be long, it was longer than expected and it was afternoon before the boat left the protection of the wharf and ventured out into the ocean. The rain was still falling and a wind had come up and the sea was choppy. The wind was off the land so they stood with their backs towards Canna and to the wind and the rain. When they were far enough out to sea to have perspective, one of the men said, "It looks like there is a fire back there." And when they looked back they could see the billowing smoke, somehow seeming ironic in the rain. It rose in the distance and was carried by the wind but it was difficult to see its source not only because of the smoke but also because of the driving rain. And because the perspective from the water was different than it was on the land. The government men did not know any of the local people and they were behind schedule and already well out to sea so there was no thought of turning back. They were mildly concerned too about the rising wind and wanted to make as much headway as possible before conditions worsened.

It was that period of the day when the afternoon blends into evening before the boat reached the Kintail wharf. During the last miles the ocean had roughened and within the rocking boat the passengers had become green and seasick and vomited their lobster sandwiches over the side. Canna seemed very far away and the golden week seemed temporarily lost within the reality of the swaying boat and the pelting rain. When the boat docked, they ran to their house as quickly as they could. Their mother gave them soup and dry clothes and they went to bed earlier than usual.

They slept late the next day and when they awoke and went downstairs it was still raining and blowing. And then the Syrian pedlars, Angus and Alex, knocked on the door. They put their heavy wet leather packs upon the kitchen floor and told the boys' mother that there had been a death in Canna. The Canna people were sending word but they had heard the news earlier in the day from another pedlar arriving from that direction and he had asked them to carry the message. The pedlars and the boys' parents talked for awhile and the boys were told to "go outside and play" even though it was raining. They went out to the barn.

Almost immediately the boys' parents began to get ready for the journey. The ocean was by this time too rough for a boat and they had already hauled their boat up at the end of the lobster season. They readied their horse and buggy and later in the afternoon they were gone. They were away for five days and when they returned they were drawn and tired.

Through bits and pieces of conversation, the boys learned that it was the blind woman's house which had burned and she within it.

Later, and they were not sure just when, they gathered other details and bits of information. She had been at the stove, it was thought, and her clothes had caught fire. The animals had burned with her. Most of their bones were found before the door to which they had gone to seek escape but she had been unable to open it for them or, it seemed, for herself.

Over the weeks the details blended in with their own experience. They imagined her strong hands pulling down the wainscotting of her own house and placing it in the fire, consuming her own house somehow from within as it was later to consume her. And they could see the fire going up the front of her layers of dirty clothing. Consuming the dirt which she herself had been unable to see. Rising up the front of her clothing, rising up above her shoulders towards her hair, the imaginary orange flames flickering and framing her face and being reflected in the staring lenses of her glasses.

And they imagined the animals too. The savage faithful dogs which were twins snarling at the doorway with their fur in flames, and the lusty cats engaged in their growling copulation in the corner, somehow keeping on, driven by their own heat while the other heat surrounded them, and the bleating lamb with its wool on fire. And in the space between the walls the mewing unseen kittens, dying with their eyes still closed.

And sometimes they imagined her too, in her porch or in her house or standing by the roadside in the rain. *Cò a th'ann?* they heard her call in their imagination and in their dreams. *Cò a th'ann? Cò a th'ann?* Who's there? Who's there? And one night they dreamed they heard themselves answer. *'Se mi-fhìn* they heard themselves say as with one voice. It is myself.

My father and his brother never again spent a week on the green hills of Canna. Perhaps their lives went by too fast or circumstances changed or there were reasons that they did not fully understand themselves.

And one Sunday six years later when they were in church the clergyman gave a rousing sermon on why young men should enlist in World War I. They were very enthusiastic about the idea and told their parents that they were going to Halifax to enlist although they were too young. Their parents were very upset and went to the clergyman in an attempt to convince him it was a mistake. The clergyman was their friend and came to their house and told them it was a general sermon for the day. "I didn't mean *you,*" he added, but his first success was better than his second.

They left the next day for Halifax, getting a ride to the nearest railroad station. They had never been on a train before and when they arrived, the city of Halifax was large and awesome. At the induction centre their age was easily overlooked but the medical examination was more serious. Although they were young and strong, the routine tests seemed strange and provoked a tension within them. They were unable to urinate in a bottle on request and were asked to wait awhile and then try again. But sitting on two chairs wishing for urine did little good. They drank more and more water and waited and tried but it did not work. On their final attempt, they were discussing their problem in Gaelic while standing in a tiny cubicle with their legs spread apart and their trousers opened.

Unexpectedly a voice from the next cubicle responded to them in Gaelic.

The voice belonged to a young man from Canna who had come to enlist as well but who did not have their problem. "Can we 'borrow' some of that?" they asked, looking at his full bottle of urine.

"Sure," he said, "no need to give it back," and he splashed some of his urine into each of their waiting bottles. All of them "passed" the test; and later in the alleyway behind the induction centre and standing in the steam of their own urine, they began to talk to the young man from Canna. His grandfather owned the store in Canna, he said, and was opposed to his coming to enlist.

"Do you know Alex?" they asked and mentioned their grandfather's formal name.

He seemed puzzled for a moment and then brightened. "Oh," he said, "*Mac an Amharuis*, sure, everyone knows him. He's my grandfather's friend."

And then, perhaps because they were far from home and more lonely and frightened than they cared to admit, they began to talk in Gaelic. They began with the subject of *Mac an Amharuis*, and the young man told them everything he knew. Surprised perhaps at his own knowledge and at having such attentive listeners. *Mac an Amharuis* translates as "Son of Uncertainty," which meant that he was illegitimate or uncertain as to who his father was. He was supposed to be tremendously talented and clever as a young man but also restless and reluctant to join the other young men of Canna in their fishing boats. Instead he saved his money and purchased a splendid stallion and travelled the country offering the stallion's services. He rode on the stallion's back with only a loose rope around its neck for guidance.

He was also thought to be handsome and to possess a "strong nature" or "too much nature," which meant that he was highly sexed. "Some say," said the young man, "that he sowed almost as much seed as the stallion and who knows who might be descended from him. If we only knew, eh?" he added with a laugh.

Then he became involved with a woman from Canna. She was thought to be "odd" by some because she was given to rages and uncertainty and sometimes she would scream and shout at him in public. At times he would bring back books and sometimes moonshine from wherever he went with the stallion. And sometimes they would read quietly together and talk and at other times they would curse and shout and become physically violent.

And then he became possessed of *Da Shealladh*, the second sight. It seemed he did not want it and some said it came about because of too much reading of the books or perhaps it was inherited from his unknown father. Once he "saw" a storm on the evening of a day which was so calm that no one would believe him. When it came in the evening the boats could not get back and all the men were drowned. And once when he was away with the stallion, he "saw" his mother's house burn down and when he returned he found that it had happened on the very night he saw it and his mother was burned to death.

It became a weight upon him and he could not stop the visions or do anything to interfere with the events. One day after he and the woman had had too much to drink they went to visit a well-known clergyman. He told the clergyman he wanted the visions to stop but it did not seem within his power. He and the woman were sitting on two chairs beside each other. The clergyman went for the Bible and prayed over it and then he came and flicked the pages of the Bible before their eyes. He told them the visions would stop but that they would have to give up one another because they were causing a scandal in the community. The woman became enraged and leaped at the clergyman and tried to scratch out his eyes with her long nails. She accused *Mac an Amharuis* of deceiving her and said that he was willing to exchange their stormy relationship for his lack of vision. She spat in his face and cursed him and stormed out the door. *Mac an Amharuis* rose to follow her but the clergyman put his arms around him and wrestled him to the floor. He was far gone in drink and within the clergyman's power.

They stopped appearing with one another and *Mac an Amharuis* stopped travelling with the stallion and bought himself a boat. He began to visit the woman's younger sister, who was patient and kind. The woman moved out of her parents' house and into an older house nearer the shore. Some thought she moved because she could not stand *Mac an Amharuis* visiting her sister, and others thought that it was planned to allow him to visit her at night without anyone seeing.

Within two months *Mac an Amharuis* and the woman's sister were married. At the wedding the woman cursed the clergyman until he warned her to be careful and told her to leave the building. She cursed her sister too and said, "You will never be able to give him what I can." And as she was going out the door, she said to *Mac an Amharuis* either "I will never forgive you" or "I will never forget you." Her voice was charged with emotion but her back was turned to them and the people were uncertain whether it was a curse or a cry.

The woman did not come near anyone for a long time and people saw her only from a distance, moving about the house and the dilapidated barn, caring for the few animals which her father had given her, and muffled in clothes as autumn turned to winter. At night people watched for a light in her window. Sometimes they saw it and sometimes they did not.

And then one day her father came to the house of his daughter and *Mac an Amharuis* and said that he had not seen a light for three nights and he was worried. The three of them went to the house but it was cold. There was no heat when they put their hands on the stove and the glass of the windowpanes was covered with frost. There was not anybody in any of the rooms.

They went out into the barn and found her lying in a heap. Most of the top part of her body was still covered by layers of clothes, although the lower part was not. She was unconscious or in something like a frozen coma and her eyes were inflamed, with beads of pus at their corners. She had given birth to twin girls and one of them was dead but the other somehow still alive, lying on her breast amidst her layers of clothing. Her father and *Mac an Amharuis* and her sister carried the living into the house and started a fire in the stove and sent for the nearest medical attention, which was some miles away. Later they also carried in the body of the dead baby and placed it in a lobster crate, which was all that they could find. When the doctor came, he said he could not be certain of the baby's exact time of birth but he felt that it would live. He said that the mother had lost a great deal of blood and he thought she might have lacerated her eyes during the birth with her long fingernails and that infection had set in, caused perhaps by the unsanitary conditions within the barn. He was not sure if she would live and, if she did, he feared her sight would never be restored.

Mac an Amharuis and his wife cared for the baby throughout the days that the woman was unconscious, and the baby thrived. The woman herself began to rally and the first time she heard the baby cry she reached out instinctively for it but could not find it in the dark. Gradually, as she recognized, by sound, the people around her, she began to curse them and accused them of having sex when she could not see them. As she grew stronger, she became more resentful of their presence and finally asked them to leave. She began to rise from her bed and walk with her hands before her, sometimes during the day and sometimes during the night because it made no difference to her. And once they saw her with a knife in her hand. They left her then, as she had requested them to do and perhaps because they were afraid. And because there seemed no other choice, they took the baby with them.

They continued to bring her food and to leave it at the door of her porch. Sometimes she cursed at them but at other times she was more quiet. One day while they were talking she extended her hand with the long fingernails to the face of *Mac an Amharuis*. She ran the balls of her fingers and the palm of her hand from his hair down over his eyes and nose and his lips and his chin and down along the buttons of his shirt and below his belt to between his legs; and then her hand closed for an instant and she grasped what she had held before but would never see again.

Mac an Amharuis and his wife had no children of their own. It was thought that it caused a great sadness within her and perhaps a tension because, as people said, "It's sure as hell not *his* fault." Their childlessness was thought also to prey on him and to lead to periodic drinking binges, although he never mentioned it to anyone. For the most part, they were helpful and supportive of each other and no one knew what they talked about when they were alone and together in their bed at night.

This, I guess, is my retelling of the story told by the young man of Canna to my father and his brother at a time when they were all young and on the verge of war. All of the information that spilled out of him came because it was there to be released and he was revealing more than he realized to his attentive listeners. The story was told in Gaelic, and as the people say, "It is not the same in English," although the images are true.

When the war was over, the generous young man from Canna was dead and my father's brother had lost his leg.

My father returned to Kintail and the life that he had left, the boat and the nets and the lobster traps. All of them in the cycle of the seasons. He married before World War II; and when he was asked to go again, he went with the other Highlanders from Cape Breton, leaving his wife pregnant, perhaps without realizing it.

On the beach at Normandy they were emptied into ten feet of water as the rockets and shells exploded around them. And in the mud they fell facedown, leaving the imprints of their faces temporarily in the soil, before clawing their way some few feet forward. At the command they rose, as would a wave trying to break farther forward on the shore. And then all of it seemed to happen at once. Before my father's eyes there rose a wall of orange flame and a billowing wave of black smoke. It rose before him even as he felt the power of the strong hand upon his left shoulder. The grip was so powerful that he felt the imprint of the fingers almost as a bruise; and even as he turned his searing eyes, he fell back into his own language. "*Cò a th'ann?*" he said. "*Cò a th'ann?* Who's there?" And in the instant before his blindness, he recognized the long brown fingers on his shoulder with their pointed fingernails caked in dirt. "*'Se mi-fhìn,*" she said quietly. "It is myself."

All of the soldiers in front of my father were killed and in the spot where he stood there was a crater, but this was told to him because he was unable ever to see it for himself.

Later he was told that on the day of his blinding, his grandfather, the man known to some as *Mac an Amharuis,* died. *Mac an Amharuis* was a man of over a hundred years at the time of his death and his eyes had become covered with the cataracts of age. He did not recognize, either by sight or sound, any of the people around him, and much of his talk was of youth and sex and of the splendid young stallion with the loose rope around its neck. And much of it was of the green island of Canna which he had never literally seen and of the people riding their horses at Michaelmas and carrying the bodies of their dead round towards the sun. And of the strong-willed St. Columba determined to be ascetic with his "back turned on Ireland" and the region of his early love. And of walls of flame and billowing smoke.

When I began this story I was recounting the story which my father told to me as he faced the green hills of Canna on the last day of the lobster season a long time ago. But when I look on it now I realize that all of it did not come from him, exactly as I have told it, on that day. The part about seeing his grandfather in the barn and much of the story of the young man from Canna came instead from his twin brother who participated in most of the events. Perhaps because of the loss of his leg, my father's brother became one of those veterans from World War I who spent a lot of their time in the Legion Hall. When he spoke to me he had none of the embarrassment which my father sometimes showed when discussing certain subjects. Perhaps my father, by omitting certain parts of his story, was merely repeating the custom of his parents who did not reveal to him at once everything there was to be shown.

But perhaps the story also went into me because of other events which happened on that day. After my father had finished, we started our engine and went into the wharf. By the time we arrived, the MacAllesters had gone and many of the other men as well. We hoisted the lobsters to the wharf's cap and I looked at the weight that the scales showed.

Whether the buyers noticed the concealed lobsters behind the crate we were never to know, but they said nothing. We unloaded our traps on the wharf and then climbed up the iron ladder and talked casually to the buyers and received our money. We planned to come back later for the lobsters behind the crate.

There were still other fishermen about and most of them shared my father's good mood because they were glad that the season had ended and pleased to have the money which was their final payment. Someone offered us a ride in a truck to the Legion and we went.

The Legion Hall was filled with men, most of them fishermen, and the noise was loud and the conversation boisterous. Towards the back of the hall I noticed Kenneth MacAllester with a number of his relatives. Both of us were underage but it did not matter a great deal. If you looked like you were old enough, no one asked any questions. My father's brother and a number of our own relatives were at a table in the middle. They waved to us and I moved towards them. Behind me, my father followed, touching my belt from time to time for guidance. Most of the men pulled in their feet as we approached so that my father would not stumble. The crutch my uncle used in place of his missing leg was propped up across a chair and he removed it as we approached and leaned it against the table so that he could offer the chair to my father. We sat down and my uncle gave me some money to go to the bar for beer. Coming back, I passed another table of MacAllesters. They were relatives of our neighbours and although I recognized them I did not know them very well. One of them said something as I passed but I did not hear what he said and it seemed best not to stop. The afternoon grew more boisterous and bottles and glasses began to shatter on the cement floor. And then there was a shower of droplets over our head.

"What's that?" said my father.

Two of the MacAllesters from the table I had passed were throwing quarts of beer to their relatives at the back of the hall. They were standing up like quarterbacks and spiralling the open quarts off the palms of their hands and I saw Kenneth reach up and catch one as if he were a wide receiver. The quarts, for the most part, stayed upright; but as they revolved and spun, their foaming contents sprinkled or drenched those seated beneath them.

"Those bastards," said my uncle.

The two of them came over to the table. They were about thirty and strong and heavily muscled.

"Who are you talking to?" one of them said.

"Never mind," said my uncle. "Go and sit down."

"I asked you a question," he said. And then turning to me he added, "I asked you a question before too. What's the matter, can't some of you hear? I just thought that some of you couldn't see."

There was a silence then that began to spread to the neighbouring tables and the conversations slowed and the men took their hands off their bottles and their glasses.

"I asked you your age," he said, still looking at me. "Are you the oldest or the youngest?"

"He's the only one," said the other man. "Since the war, his father is so blind he can't find his way into his wife's cunt to make any more."

I remember my uncle reaching for the bottom of his crutch, and he swung it like a baseball bat from his sitting position. And I remember the way he planted his one leg onto the floor even as he swung. And I remember the crutch exploding into the nose and mouth of the man and his blood splashing down upon us and then the overturning of tables and chairs and the crashing of broken glass. And I remember also two of the MacAllesters who were our neighbours reaching our table with amazing speed. Each of them went to a side of my father's chair and they lifted it up with him still sitting upon it. And they carried him as carefully as if he were eggs or perhaps an object of religious veneration, and the men who were smashing their fists into one another's mouths moved out of their way when they saw them coming. They deposited him with great gentleness against the far wall where they felt no harm could come to him, bending their knees in unison as they lowered his chair to the floor. And then each of them placed a hand upon his shoulder as one might comfort a frightened child. And then one of them picked up a chair and smashed it over the head of my cousin who had his brother by the throat.

Someone grabbed me and spun me around but I could see by his eyes that he was intent on someone across the hall and that I was merely in his way. And then I saw Kenneth coming towards me, as I half expected him to. It was like the bench clearing brawls at the hockey games when the goalies seek each other out because they have the most in common.

I saw him coming with his eyes intent upon me and because I knew him well I believed that he would leap from a spot about three strides ahead of him and that the force of his momentum would carry us backwards and I would be on the bottom with my head on the cement floor. It all took perhaps a fraction of a second, his leap and my bending and moving forward and sideways, either to go towards him or to get out of the way, and my shoulder grazing his hip as he was airborne with his hands stretched out before him and his body parallel to the floor. He came crashing down on top of the table, knocking it over and forward and beneath him to the cement.

He lay facedown and still for a moment and I thought he was unconscious and then I saw the blood spreading from beneath his face and reddening the shards of different-coloured glass.

"Are you all right?" I said, placing my hand upon his shoulder.

"It's okay," he said. "It's just my eye."

He sat up then with his hands over his face and the blood streaming down between his fingers. I was aware of a pair of rubber boots beside us and then a man's voice. "Stop," he shouted to the brawling hall. "For Christ's sake, stop, someone's been hurt."

In retrospect, and even then, it seemed like a strange thing to say because when one looked at the bloodied men it seemed that almost everyone had been hurt in some way, although not to the same degree. But given the circumstances, he said exactly the right thing and everyone stopped and unclenched his fist and released his grip on his opponent's throat.

In the rush to the doctor and to the hospital, everyone's original plans went awry. No one thought of the lobsters we had hidden and saved for our end-of-the-season feast; and when we discovered them days later, it was with something like surprise. They were dead and had to be thrown back into the sea, perhaps to serve as food for the spring mackerel with the scales upon their eyes.

That night two cars of MacAllesters came to our house. They told us that Kenneth's eye was lost; and Mr. MacAllester, who was about my father's age, began to cry. The two young men who were throwing the beer held their caps in their hands and their knuckles were still raw and bleeding. Both of them apologized to my father. "We didn't see it getting that out of hand," one of them said. My uncle came in from another room and said that he shouldn't have swung the crutch.

Mr. MacAllester said that if my father would agree, all of us should stop using the fickle river as the boundary between our fishing grounds and take our sightings instead from the two rocky promontories on either side of the beach. One family would fish off the beach one year and the other the next. My father agreed. "I can't see the boundary anyway," he said with a smile. It all seemed so simple in hindsight.

This has been the telling of a story about a story but like most stories it has spun off into others and relied on others and perhaps no story ever really stands alone. This began as the story of two children who long ago went to visit their grandparents but who, because of circumstances, did not recognize them when they saw them. As their grandparents did not see them. And this is a story related by a man who is a descendant of those people. The son of a father who never saw his son but knew him only through sound or by the running of his fingers across the features of his face.

As I write this, my own small daughter comes in from kindergarten. She is at the age where each day she asks a riddle and I am not supposed to know the answer. Today's question is, "What has eyes but cannot see?" Under the circumstances, the question seems overwhelmingly profound. "I don't know," I say and I feel I really mean it.

"A potato," she shouts and flings herself into my arms,

enthused and impressed by her own cleverness and by my lack of understanding.

She is the great-great-granddaughter of the blind woman who died in flames and of the man called *Mac an Amharuis;* and both of us, in spite of our age and comprehension, are indeed the children of uncertainty.

Most of the major characters in this story are, as the man called *Mac an Amharuis* once said of others, "all gone" in the literal sense. There remains only Kenneth MacAllester, who works as a janitor for a soap company in Toronto. Unable ever to join the Air Force and fly towards the sun and see over the tops of mountains and across the ocean because of what happened to his eye on that afternoon so long ago. Now he has an artificial eye and, as he says, "Only a few people know the difference."

When we were boys we would try to catch the slippery spring mackerel in our hands and look into the blindness of their eyes, hoping to see our own reflections. And when the wet ropes of the lobster traps came out of the sea, we would pick out a single strand and then try to identify it some few feet farther on. It was difficult to do because of the twisting and turning of the different strands within the rope. Difficult to be ever certain in our judgements or to fully see or understand. Difficult then to see and understand the twisted strands within the rope. And forever difficult to see and understand the tangled twisted strands of love.

Afterword

BY JANE URQUHART

Each time I read the stories in *As Birds Bring Forth the Sun and Other Stories* I am struck by the largeness of Alistair MacLeod's main characters. This is not only a largeness of physical stature but also, and more important, a largeness of soul, a generosity of spirit. Reflective and emotional without being self-conscious, his men are intimate, not just with women and children, but with the rough beauty of their geography, the old sorrows of their family legends, the sanctity of work, the mating cycles and slaughter of their animals; in short, with life itself. Although the presence of the "anima" in general is strong and benign in these stories, they are really about the masculine spirit, its strengths and its vulnerabilities. Time and again we are put in mind of the old Celtic heroes, of Oisin arguing ethics with Saint Patrick or of Finn McCool mourning the loss of his beloved dog Bran. And yet, at the same time, we are brought into closer contact with the men who are part of our own world and who are our friends and our family.

Like many other Canadians of Irish or Scottish background, MacLeod himself was brought up in the midst of a tribal, Celtic family much given to remembering the past and measuring the present in terms of it. In such families the tales of previous generations are told spontaneously and repetitively as a means of establishing both geographically and emotionally where the family has been, where it is now, and where it is going. In MacLeod's fiction the "voice" of the oral tradition is never far away and in some cases is as close as the opening sentences of a story. "Once there was a family with a Highland name who lived beside the sea," we are told in "As Birds Bring Forth the Sun." "And the man had a dog of which he was very fond." In the space of a few short sentences we, the readers, have joined the family, have entered the rooms of their houses, and have gathered together to hear the remainder of the tale. By the time the story is finished, the identification is so complete that we feel the hair rising on the backs of our own necks and hear the claws of the *cù mòr glas*, the big grey dog, scratching at our own doors. Moreover, a brilliant transformation has taken place. By skilfully interweaving past and present, recurring images and sensual detail, MacLeod creates a complex tapestry out of a seemingly simple and much-told family tale.

MacLeod's stories have been called – albeit with great admiration – traditional, even conservative, by a literary world cluttered with theories and "isms." They are, however, in their portrayal of an ancestral past that continually affects the present and in their sense of deep yearning for forsaken landscapes, as fresh and as complex as the present moment. We Canadians are, after all, a nation composed of people longing for a variety of abandoned homelands and the tribes that inhabited them, whether these be the distant homelands of our recent immigrants, the abducted homelands of our native peoples, the rural homelands vacated by the post-war migrations to the cities, or the various European or Asian homelands left behind by our earliest settlers. All of us have been touched in some way or another by this loss of landscape and of kin, and all of us are moved by the sometimes unidentifiable sorrow that accompanies such a loss. We are also moved, however, by the comfort we are afforded when an artist of the calibre of Alistair MacLeod carries such sorrowful and penetrating themes towards us in his gentle and capable hands.

These themes are not only Canadian ones, of course, they are universal – migration having been always a part of the human experience – and in MacLeod's stories, as in all great art, the universal becomes clearer and sharper when we are brought into intimate contact with the particular. I am always impressed, for instance, by the tension MacLeod creates in this country of vast distances and brutal weather by the antici-pated journey home. A young man wishing to return to Cape Breton for Christmas from a job on Ontario lake freighters is dependent on the Great Lakes freezing, on the one hand, and on the highways being free of crippling blizzards on the other. A boy relies on a golden dog to guide him towards his warm kitchen and away from his death on a partly frozen sea. A crew of shaft and development miners knows that if one of them dies underground, as is so often the case, his comrades will make the dangerous winter journey to ferry the broken body back to the ancestral graveyard. A group of scattered relatives is aware that they will attempt to drive the long highways home to attend the funeral of a loved one despite the fear that the journey will be rendered impossible by winter, circum-stance, change, or the fact that the return itself may be almost too painful to be borne. As the exiled narrator in "Winter Dog" laments:

> Should we be forced to drive tonight, it will be a long,
> tough journey into the wind and the driving snow which
> is pounding across Ontario and Quebec and New
> Brunswick and against the granite coast of Nova Scotia.
> Should we be drawn by death, we might well meet
> our own.

And in the middle of the long, multi-layered, and disturbing story entitled "Vision," the grandfather quotes the poem

reputed to have been uttered thirteen hundred years ago by
Saint Colum Cille upon his exile from Ireland:

> *There is a grey eye*
> *Looking back on Ireland,*
> *That will never see again*
> *Her men or her women.*
>
> *Early and late my lamentation,*
> *Alas, the journey I am making;*
> *This will be my secret bye-name*
> *"Back turned on Ireland."*

MacLeod's stories are resonant with the lamentations of
exiles, and strong within these lamentations is the desire to
preserve that which was, and even that which is, against the
heartbreaking ravages of time; to preserve, not necessarily
with factual accuracy, but rather with something that one can
only call, trite though it sounds, emotional truth. Like the
fishermen in "Vision" and in the interests of this goal,
MacLeod defines his boundaries by making use of "the actual
river" when it suits his purposes or, when it does not, "an earlier imaginary river which [he] can no longer see." Hence a
tale from the past sheds as much clear light on a character or a
situation as a contemporary word or deed and, in the end,
preservation is accomplished by establishing the timelessness
of legend.

To explore timelessness, preservation, and emotional truth
is among the purest of literary intentions and, because of this,
the seven stories in *As Birds Bring Forth the Sun and Other
Stories* seem to move effortlessly from the author's heart to the
page and then to leap back from the page into the heart of the
reader. This is not to suggest that there is anything resembling
a "stream-of-consciousness" approach in the writing. In fact,
MacLeod is so "care-full," in the true sense of the word, that
quite the opposite is true. All of the stories have been "tuned to

perfection" both technically and emotionally and with such care that they burst into sensual life as we read. We see and feel the cold, wet nose of a beloved dog, the delicate form of an embryo calf exposed within the slaughtered body of its mother, captured lobsters moving awkwardly on the floor of a fishing boat. But, most important, we are witness to a deepness of caring that reveals itself with brutality and tenderness, a deepness of caring that binds man to woman, father to son, man to animal, and humanity to kin and landscape.

The depth of caring that is examined in *As Birds Bring Forth the Sun* is as much active as it is reflective in its expression. All of the protagonists are men whose lives are inexorably bound to the physical: the netting of fish, the husbandry of animals, the carving of rock from the bowels of the earth. Almost immediately the reader comes to trust the heavy, muscular presence of such men who in many cases carry the history of their physicality around with them in the form of wounds or scars. Even the entry of a family story concerning old sorrows into the mind and memory of a young man is described actively, physically, and compared to wounds and scars. "You know," says the narrator in "Vision," "the future scar will be forever on the outside while the memory will remain, forever, deep within." By associating memory with blood and body, MacLeod suggests that emotion is biological and genetic and can never, therefore, be connected to that which is ephemeral or casual.

In the end it is this utter absence of the casual that gives MacLeod's stories their enormous power and raises them to the level of myth. "Second Spring" is much more than the tale of a Maritime boy "smitten with the calf club wish." It reaches back through time to all the sacred bulls and cows that have existed in Celtic, Greek, and Eastern myth. The *cù mòr glas*, which in the title story operates, for one family, as a sort of canine banshee, is equally Finn McCool's great dog Bran loping across the Giant's Causeway from Ireland to Scotland and

Charon's dog Cerebus guarding the gates to the underworld and keeping watch over the River Styx. In "Vision" references to second sight, blindness, memory, and a constant shifting of understanding call to mind the blindfolded figure of justice and cause us to examine the nature of perception itself.

One winter night I was fortunate enough to hear Alistair MacLeod read from new fiction. I took home from that evening images of knives and forks being placed on a kitchen floor by children playing store, a nocturnal winter landscape viewed through glass, and, in the distance, one lantern going dark and another coming to rest far out on the ice. Like the old masters in W. H. Auden's "Musée des Beaux Arts," MacLeod is never wrong about suffering and understands "how it takes place / While someone else is eating or opening a window or just walking dully along;" or "how everything turns away / Quite leisurely from the disaster." But it is not the leisurely turning away that commands the focus of MacLeod's attention. Somewhere around the middle of the piece he read that night, he described a dog whose passion leads him to a tragedy as final as the one that visited his lantern-carrying owners. Someone, a grandfather I believe, says, "It was in those dogs to care too much, to try too hard," meaning that this exaggerated trying and caring was bred into such dogs in Scotland over 150 years ago. Sitting in the audience and hearing that line, I was suddenly convinced that MacLeod was describing not only a certain breed of dog but all of his characters, animal and human, and the writer himself, engaged in his craft.

This is what we want from our best authors: not merely that they care and try but that they care *too* much and try *too* hard, that the intensification of feeling and of meaning manifests itself in their hearts and in their work. We come away from the stories in *As Birds Bring Forth the Sun and Other*

Stories with that desire completely satisfied, our own world view intensified, enlarged, and enriched. And we come away understanding more clearly "the twisted strands within the rope," the difficult, "tangled twisted strands of love."

BY ALISTAIR MACLEOD

FICTION
The Lost Salt Gift of Blood (1976)
As Birds Bring Forth the Sun and Other Stories (1986)
No Great Mischief (1999)
Island (2000)

Acknowledgements

The stories listed below originally appeared in the following publications:

"The Closing Down of Summer" in *The Fiddlehead*, Number 111, Fall 1976; reprinted in *Fiddlehead Greens: Stories from the Fiddlehead*, Oberon, 1979. "Winter Dog" in *Canadian Fiction Magazine*, Number 40/41, 1981. "To Every Thing There Is a Season" in the *Globe and Mail*, December 24, 1977. "Second Spring" in *Canadian Fiction Magazine*, Number 34/35, 1980. "The Tuning of Perfection" in *The Cape Breton Collection*, Pottersfield Press, Nova Scotia, 1984. "As Birds Bring Forth the Sun" in *event* magazine, Volume 14, Number 2, 1985.

I would like to thank Kerstin Mueller of the Eastern Counties Regional Libraries and Roddie Coady of the Coady and Tompkins Memorial Library for providing me with much-needed and much-appreciated writing space.

I would also like to thank A. G. MacLeod, Murdina Stewart and the University of Windsor for their different kinds of help and cooperation. The translations of the longer Gaelic songs are from *Beyond the Hebrides* (1977), edited by Donald A. Fergusson. Again, my thanks.